SCION OF THE EMPIRE

Red Dawn III

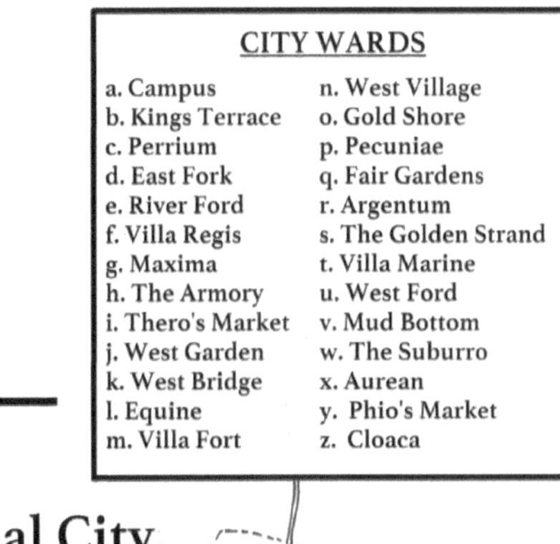

Imperial City, 210 Y.E.

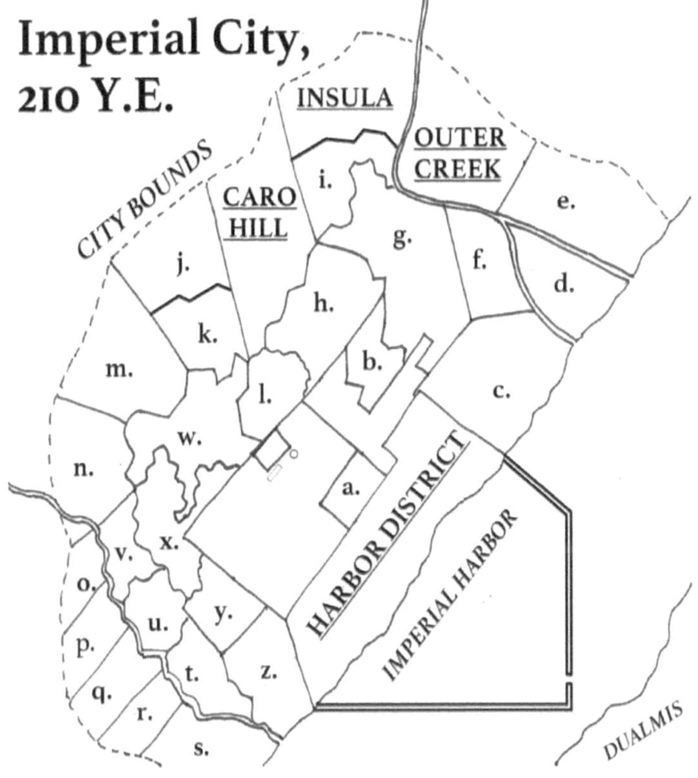

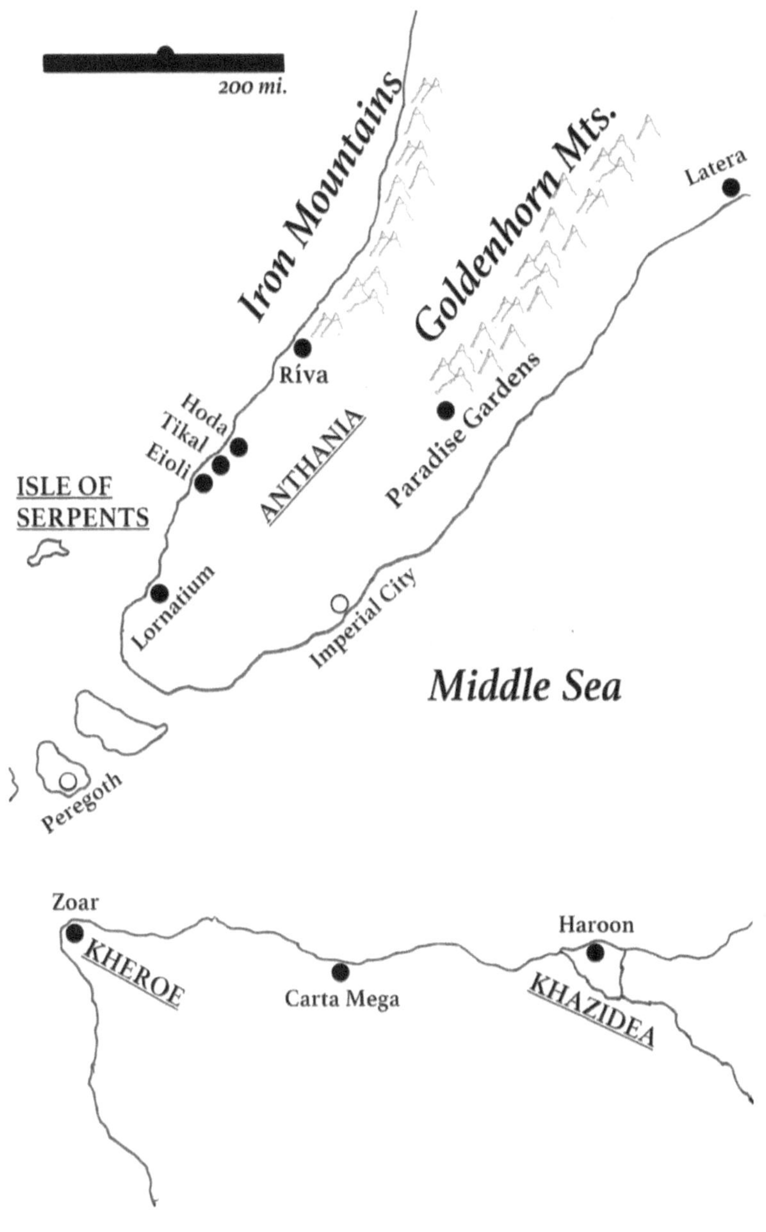

200 mi.
Iron Mountains
Goldenhorn Mts.
Latera
Ríva
Hoda
Tikal
Eioli
ISLE OF SERPENTS
ANTHANIA
Paradise Gardens
Lornatium
Imperial City
Middle Sea
Peregoth
Zoar
KHEROE
Carta Mega
Haroon
KHAZIDEA

The Decree

From his seat on the White Throne, the emperor made his decree: that the Empire shall consist of the peninsula and the City, and nothing more… that it shall not expand; that if the men and women of Eioli give up their arms, they shall not be harmed.

But news troubled him, news from the far corners but most of all news close to home: Julia, the one he loved, was gone…

Part One

Chapter One

Aulus Meridius, Centurion

For months he had looked upon those hateful walls, the walls of Eioli, proud and insolent, colored gold. He had heard of the city's many horrors, and he had seen its wealth. Aulus Meridius, the leader of the Red Century, had set his heart against it.

He watched as more legionaries poured in, legionaries from across the sea and far away, from the north. But he turned to see Eioli, and there was wrath in his heart.

The city had claimed the life of a good man, Varius Tycho, his friend. The city had claimed the life of Agatho Lornodoris, commander-in-chief, in the most treacherous of ways.

And Aulus Meridius, leader of the Red Century, husband of Falernia, father of Claudia and Horatius, knew his wrath was building, that it was beginning to take root, that it was beginning to take control of him.

And so he marched up to Eioli's towering city gates. Legionaries turned to look and so he had an audience.

He drew from his sheath his sword. He cut open his fingers and let the blood drip.

The rite he was performing was not Imperial, nor was the god to whom it was consecrated. It was foreign, but it had been done before.

"Men of the Red Century, of the Sixth Anthanian, of the Second Peregothian and all others…"

The dark spirits that haunted Eioli had driven the legions away, but only a little while; the legions had become accustomed to the Ugars' dirty tricks.

The legionaries of the Empire, stunned but for a moment, had returned to the site of the siege, and the defenders on the walls of Eioli had wailed.

Aulus' audience was captive; the legionaries' eyes were twinkling in anticipation. His fingers continued to dribble blood.

"The Rite of Devotion I perform," Aulus said. "If Yblis, the god of the underworld, grants me victory, then I will sacrifice my life to the chthonic host. If Eioli falls, I will offer myself as his prize."

The legionaries looked appalled; centurions and tribunes were watching with mouths agape. There was no going back now.

But so great was his wrath that he would do anything to see the city fall. So great was his wrath that he was willing to do this, to perform the Rite of Devotion.

And so it was seen; and so it was done. There was no abandoning his promise. Aulus Meridius, leader of the Red Century, husband of Falernia, father of Claudia and Horatius, had pledged his life to Eioli's fall. All was in Yblis' hands now.

Chapter Two

Julia Seánus

How many times had she retreated here?

She was away from the city, ten miles from its outer bounds, in Herne's Glade, in the Chrysum Forest.

She had been to this glade before, to meditate, to escape.

And now she was doing both. Because she was afraid.

She was afraid, not of Varro, not of the supposedly ferocious Ugars. No, she was afraid of the Imperial Council, and of herself.

She had told the government the location of Varro's lair. Mass arrests were underway in Imperial City. The Red Hand cult was about to be stamped out for good.

And she had been a member. She would be under the eyes of the law; yes, the law that not even the Seánus family was above. For the eyes of Lady Justice were blind, and she did not care for August or common or Knight.

How beautiful were these oaks. There was a promise of spring.

Green was the grass in Herne's Glade, and the blades gleamed with dew. Deer were here in abundance, here in the highlands. Chrysum had been her favorite place of all as a girl. And now she was returning to that vulnerable place, the place she had been before the storms of adolescence and adulthood, the storms that had brought her to where she was now.

Publius was surely worried sick. But she was safe and unharmed, at least for now.

She had seen the ring he had bought her.

He had been common; the Imperial Council had named him August. And now, vested in him were unthinkable powers, the powers to make war, to carry out justice, to set policy… and responsibilities as well, responsibilities that were just as unthinkable: to protect the nation, to lead its armies in war, to maintain the confidence of the Council.

Was he up for it? Julia had an inkling that he was.

Birds were singing. The leaves of the oaks were green. The sun was shining in the blue sky, and Julia, in this moment, could feel the happy wind of spring.

How beautiful were these woods, how gentle. The forests of her homeland, of the peninsula, were benign and inviting, even welcoming. Where the forests of the north were harsh and full of danger—threatening wind and snow and hunger—here, in Anthania, where she had been born, where she would stay, she felt at peace. In her father's military campaigns she had seen the terrors of the north. She would not dwell there.

She sat down in Herne's Glade and felt the grass moisten her gown.

She called up her powers, allowed the magic to percolate, allowed it to infuse her. Then she shut her eyes… she reached out, as if grasping for something. She uttered the word "Publius" to focus herself and envisioned him.

And there he was, in the Imperial Council halls. He was arguing with the Speaker, Councilor Lychicus. He seemed animated.

It was not a good time to talk, to let him know she was all right. And so she relinquished her power, felt its coldness leave her, and she was back again in Herne's Glade amid the green grass… safe for now, but in the knowledge that the law was bearing down on her.

Varro's trial was set to begin. And on that occasion, everything that she had endeavored to hide would spill out for the whole world to see.

Yes, Varro's trial would be deadly for her, deadly indeed,

and though she could not and would not escape the law, here she was, in the sanctuary of her childhood, here, amid the singing of the bluebirds, here, amid the promise of spring.

Herne's Glade overlooked a great valley and beneath her the oaks sprawled into the horizon. The smoky haze of the city was visible but she was in nature, free of the city's cares and worries.

She would return. Yes, she would return.

But first a little peace was in order, a little escape.

No. I will not return… I will flee across the sea. I will take refuge in the Eastern Kingdoms. Prince Pagon will not let them have me.

Escaping to her friend Pagon's palace, in the Kingdom of Thenoa, would be a coward's way out.

Perhaps, I am a coward.

Pagon had been her father's foremost Eastern ally. He would not let harm come to Julia, though she was not a girl anymore, but a woman full grown. She had spent a summer in the richness of his palace. Would he remember her?

A coward's way out. A coward.

She turned, peering into the horizon. Her heart began to flutter; she felt disoriented, light-headed. She felt a growing dread.

And so she arose; she stiffened her back. Her stamina had grown over years of using her powers. What was it that troubled her? She was facing west by northwest.

The skies were blue. Clouds drifted by. And she sensed fear and worry. She sensed dread.

~

In her projected form she was flying, soaring faster than an eagle. She was hurtling over fields and beyond hills and green forests. She was soaring overhead of towns and villages and hamlets, over fortresses made of rock, over sprawling farms and vineyards that lay in the sun.

Soon she was near the coast, near the haunting feeling, and her dread was growing, molting into outright fear.

And amid a land of dark silt, of melons growing on vines and endless fields of wheat, beyond the shade of stone pines, she saw what it was she sensed.

A group of men were standing there in the clearing. Brush hid them from clear view.

They were swart and dark eyed, these men—Ugars but tall for Ugars. There was a man among them wearing a fish hat on his head who bore in his hands a rod—that man, a priest no doubt, was chanting.

From the wet, muddy earth something emerged… a hoof.

She sensed the priest's name was Drubal.

Another hoof emerged from the moist, muddy ground.

And then the creature wrested itself from its tomb… if a bull, the largest of all bulls. It was covered in iron-like scales. Two great horns emerged from its head. Its eyes glowed like embers and when it exhaled it puffed out green vapor.

For a moment, Julia was sick with fear, sick with disgust. But she braced herself and despite her trembling she continued to watch.

"It is ready," Drubal said. "It is like the days of old."

The metal bull jerked toward Drubal as if to gore him, but at that moment Drubal's men sank either side of the beast's mouth with iron hooks and pulled with all their might.

The bull wheezed and cried and the green vapor was like a cloud rising to the heavens. But then it was relented, and it was controlled.

Drubal had begun to laugh.

And Julia, watching, could feel something come over her, not dread, not terror, but alarm… alarm at what was occurring, alarm. She looked to the north and remembered the city of Eioli; she could feel a monster yearning, striving to break free.

And she looked again at the hideous scaled bull. Her heart said, "Run." And another thought came to her: "Bulls… Great Bulls of Phaegor!"

She relinquished her power, and she had never been so happy to be far away, never so happy to be in Herne's Glade. But she knew that though the war was far-off, if it was not won it would come close.

She asked the gods to watch over the Empire's soldiers. She asked for peace, but she knew it was a calm before the storm.

Chapter Three

Marcus Corvus

For Marcus, the trial of Tidus Sulpicius Varro promised to be the show of the century.

Who would have thought that the Marshal of the Imperial Guard was a member of a cult? Who would have thought, moreover, that he would lead it?

Marcus had taken his seat on the bench.

The past few weeks had been wild, and in all, he was not totally convinced it was not a dream. He had tried to pinch himself several times over the past few days. His brother, the emperor? His brother, whom he had teased and picked on in his youth? And by rights of his elevation, Marcus himself—and all the Corvi—were Augusts.

The trial was taking place in Legate's Square. Benches were set up and Marcus, as an August, had a front-row seat.

Neither the magistrate nor the defender had arrived.

But Tidus Sulpicius Varro had… yes, Varro had shown up. He was sitting behind a metal fence in what almost looked like a cage. He looked thin and pale, and his eyes were weak. The beginnings of a beard were on his cheeks; perhaps, he had not been allowed to shave.

He did not look like a member of the Imperial Guard at all, though Marcus did not know what an Imperial Guard was supposed to look like.

"Begin," he wanted to shout, "Begin!" But he knew trials were not meant for entertainment, but to deliver justice. The entertainment was only an unintended effect.

It was amazing, the crowds behind him and the crowds ahead of him. Marcus had found his seat at dawn, waiting with eagerness. It seemed all of Imperial City had attended, at least, those who could squeeze into the benches and those who had brought chairs of their own.

And yet as he stood there, he could not help but notice his fingers trembling. This was his third day without spice. A splitting headache afflicted him; when he looked into the mirror his eyes were glassy and when he walked he was dizzy.

But he had decided to make a change. He had grand plans.

~

"Tidus Sulpicius Varro, former Marshal of the Guard," the magistrate began. "You are hereby charged with organizing the murder of fifty-seven citizens, for which the penalty is death. How do you plead?"

Marcus had been in the city on the Day of the Knives, and like that all sympathy for Tidus Sulpicius Varro vanished. There was no sympathy left for him, none left for Marcus to give. His old friend Caecillia had died in the attack. How many others had been killed? How many families had been shattered?

"Innocent, Your Honor," answered Tidus Sulpicius Varro.

There were scattered jeers in the crowd and a few shouted words. But Tidus Sulpicius Varro seemed unmoved. The judge made a motion; the magistrate retreated to his seat.

The defender walked up to the judge. "My signores and signoras," he said. "Tidus Sulpicius Varro pledged his life to the nation. And in only one way could he work against it; he was put under a spell by Julia Seánus."

At the mention of the former emperor's daughter there were gasps. Marcus couldn't believe the strategy. It was so unlikely it beggared belief.

"For Julia Seánus, you see, was a member of the cult," the defender said. "She was a highly ranked member of the Order of the Red Hand."

Was this truly what they were staking Tidus Sulpicius Varro's life on? This argument would not be believed.

"Proof," the defender said and reached into the folds of his pocket. He drew out a necklace on which gleamed a white gem. "The Star of Seladora, the Seánus family amulet, which Julia had given Signor Varro as a gift."

How easy would it be to visit the jeweler, to have him fashion a similar necklace. Marcus had already heard enough.

~

The breeze was blowing in from Harbor District. The skies had been red at dawn and now clouds were blowing in from the sea. A storm seemed to be promised.

But as Marcus drew near Flavia's house, he noted signs had been nailed in various places along the street: "Spurius Arappo for Councilor."

He remembered the death of Agatho Lornodoris, Harbor District's councilor. The news of the Speaker's murder by the Ugars had been the talk of the town for days.

Spurius Arappo… he was an August, the lucky man.

I keep forgetting.

Marcus Corvus was August now.

How he had envied, how he had striven.

And now his dreams were at his fingertips. Could he? Would he? Did he have what it took?

Marcus Corvus, August, would declare for Harbor District. His heart gave him no other choice.

Chapter Four

Julia Seánus

She felt a foreign hand on her star.

Yes, the Star of Seladora she had called it. It was believed to be the Seánus family gem. But it had come from her mother's family, from the House of Ajax.

And into it she had placed her essence. The augurs put their essences into their staffs, the flamens into their veils. Placing one's essence was common to all forms of sorcery.

And she could sense it, though it was far.

When Varro cast her out of the cult, he had taken her star from her.

She could only imagine who was touching the star, though whoever it was was far away, and she sensed guile in his heart.

She knew the trial of Varro was ongoing.

But her mind had by now turned to other things, not to Varro, not even to Publius. She feared Eioli. She feared its monster, whatever it was.

And the Imperial Council, and she herself, did not seem so frightening anymore.

She knew her powers could help the Empire. Still, she was hesitant; still she was unsure. But sensing that monster, whatever it was, screaming, scratching, bucking to break free... it was otherworldly, that monster, not seen by human eyes. It was hideous and deadly.

And so she focused once more. Though she was without her star, she reached deep within herself. She enveloped herself in the magic.

And she soared once again across field and fen, above town and village and hamlet, and soon enough she was back in that place in her projected form; she was back in the place of rich dark silt and at the mighty gates of the city of Eioli.

~

Legions were encamped around the city walls, thousands and thousands of soldiers from all over the peninsula and the isles. Handsome they were, healthy, and they were handsomely attired as well, with polished iron breastplates and helms topped with red crests. Mixed among them were various weapons of siege, but in the wan afternoon light there was stillness. The defenders on the walls, darkly arrayed in armor, were standing silently.

The siege had not, in earnest, begun.

Julia in her projected form felt herself rising of her own accord. She flew above the walls and glimpsed the city below… flat-roofed homes and shops, market squares of dark stone. The architecture was unlike anything she'd seen, with harsh angles and grim gray stone.

But fear was rising in her, and when she looked up she saw why. She gasped as she saw Eioli's temple, mounted above the city on a high hill. It was like a tower thrice the width of the Imperial Palace, of dark smoke-stained stone, and crowned with a panoply of spires and rising turrets.

And in that temple the monster lived.

Yes, the monster lived there, the monster yearning to break free.

It lived within that tower, within that tower of dark stone and dark spires.

It was within.

Julia felt herself being pulled; she had lost control. She was being drawn in.

Soon she was sucked through a dark window, though she strained to free herself. The pull was impossible to reverse.

And in the dungeon of the tower she saw it, a shadowy form with a head like that of a bull, and two great bulbous yellow eyes.

She sensed, with terror, that it was not of this earth.

But as she drew near, she could feel the hold begin to relinquish.

Her reflection in his eyes was that of a shadowy figure staring at his hands.

The monstrous being screamed and Julia was catapulted away, across fen and field, abovehead of village and hamlet and town, until she was back in Herne's Glade, back where she had been.

She was standing there, in the cold, and in the rain.

Winter had suddenly returned to the Chrysum Forest. A harsh wind was blowing.

And that monstrous being in the dungeon of the temple was afraid of her.

It was afraid.

Chapter Five

Marcus Corvus

Election… votes…

It was what he had dreamt of in his youth, though it had been unavailable to him as a common man.

In the main hall of Flavia and Demetrius's house, he announced his plans.

"You're serious," Demetrius said, though Marcus could not tell if it was a question or a statement.

"Oh," said Flavia, "it is what you always wanted. You always used to talk about it.

"And yet… and yet…"

"And yet what?" said Marcus.

"Never mind," Flavia said instantly. "I will support you, brother, and I'll make sure Demetrius does as well."

The morning light was shining through the windows, and against the divans and tables odd shadows were forming, one, he noted, that looked like a bull.

He recalled the dreams he'd had when he smoked spice, the dreams that he was growing horns on his head, the feelings of terror that he had woken up to.

And as he lingered there in the main hall, he wondered and he waited.

Chapter Six

Aulus Meridius, Centurion

With cries of exhaustion, the soldiers of the legion were heaping dirt on dirt.

The grand legate Hastatus had ordered fortifications to be built, to close off Eioli from the outside world, for reports were circulating that an alliance of Ugar cities was marching forth to break the siege.

Tikal, Hoda, and other minor settlements had gathered their armies.

With a sally they hoped to scatter the Imperial armies to the winds.

But Aulus and the other men had seen the Ugars' dirty tricks. They were prepared to fight. They were prepared to die to see Eioli fall.

But a thought was in his head, a thought growing, one he couldn't shake. And it was one that he felt the grand legate Hastatus had to know.

He wiped his sweaty brow. His hands and legs were covered in sweat and dirt. The mounds were growing; other legionaries were hammering in palisades.

He would be gone only a little while, but perhaps much longer.

For he had ideas, ideas he wished to share.

~

As he walked he could see the legionaries hard at work. Twice, minor sallies of cavalry from the people of Eioli had tried to disrupt the construction.

But these palisade walls, carved of fire-treated wood, would do more than fortify the legion's position. They would also keep Eioli isolated, alone, without hope of escape. Nothing could go in or out.

That, at least, was what people thought.

The legate welcomed him in. His tent was spare and unornamented, little better than the other soldiers.

Hastatus was a man of the military, full and true, and had more years in its service than Aulus.

But some called him a politician. Some believed him to be false.

"Signor Aulus," Hastatus said. "I could not refuse your request for a meeting. After all, it is you who crept into Eioli and found its gold."

The reconnaissance mission had indeed found gold in Eioli's walls, but about that Aulus was not proud, for the Empire was supposed to be more than robbers.

Aulus knelt. "Signore," he said.

"Rise," Hastatus answered.

He was steely eyed, brown haired, with ruddy skin. A deep scar was over his cheek and forehead which he claimed he had earned in a battle in Kheroe. He had a wife in Imperial City, a humble house in Harbor District—or so he claimed. He was the legate of the Sixth Anthanian Legion, and grand legate of all forces fighting Eioli.

"Signore," Aulus said again, "I believe your strategy is ill advised."

"And why is that?" Hastatus said. If he was angry he showed no sign of it.

As he had surveyed the palisades being hammered into the ground, he had remembered his experience, but above all he had remembered history.

"Because we are hemming ourselves in, too," Aulus said.

"We will not be able to run. We will have no mobility."

"We cannot flee," Hastatus said. "That is what you mean."

"Not exactly," Aulus wanted to say but he kept silent. He had spoken his piece. He was a centurion and not even of Hastatus' legion. He could do no more than advise.

And perhaps it played a part in what he meant, for he feared the Ugars as much as he despised them.

"Aulus Meridius, leader of the Red Century," Hastatus began. "I was looking for a man of character, one who dares to speak his mind even at risk. Perhaps, you will do…"

~

The mission Hastatus explained was simple, so simple it worried Aulus.

"Go," said Hastatus, "take your century. With you I will send a guide to a place called Devil's Dolmen. There, if the mission is not obvious enough, my guide will tell you all you need to know."

The Red Century departed in the early morning, just before the legions sealed off the palisade wall and prevented all escape. There was no going back now, for them or for anyone.

Chapter Seven

Marcus Corvus

When Marcus Corvus announced his intention before the ward legate, there was confusion writ on his features.

"Corvus," he said, "is not a name I recognize."

"But I am August."

The legate chamber in the ward hall was of dark basalt. Crude columns crowned each corner. Behind the desk were rows and rows of books.

"You intend to stand for Harbor District," the ward legate repeated, as if in disbelief.

Marcus Corvus was young for a councilor, barely meeting the requirement of thirty. But he was qualified in every respect, and no one could deny him.

The ward legate retreated to his library.

He returned in the affirmative, with a sour look on his face as if he were disappointed. And so it was official: there was a new candidate in Harbor District.

But Marcus Corvus had fallen ill.

~

By the time he exited the ward hall, he was almost staggering. The fresh air helped only slightly. He did not understand the sickness that had seized him.

His hands were trembling. He was filled with fear.

Some in the crowds of Harbor District were staring at him, but he continued staggering on.

He did not know what he was running from, but he was fleeing from something.

At last he found himself in a market square with more space, and a fountain in the center. He keeled over and laid his hands on the stone.

He peered into his reflection and for a moment saw the head of a bull, a bull with great black eyes and a ring of gold in its nose.

Chapter Eight

Julia Seánus

In the light wind and rain, Julia descended from Herne's Glade. The Chrysum Forest was in the highlands of the Hollow Hills. It was lovely in the summertime, but now the weather had turned fierce, and it seemed winter would return in all its harshness.

She had been in this place for days, amid these trees and pools. She had tried to gather her bearings.

And still the remembrance of the monster was in her, still its eyes in which she had seen an inky reflection.

And she sensed, moreover, that it was not just the legions that were in danger, but the entire Empire.

But as she descended down the many roads of the Chrysum Forest, the memory of the monster began to weaken.

She began to think of Publius, the soldier of the Empire with whom she had fallen in love.

She retreated under the shade of an oak tree.

She called up her power.

~

Soaring through the air in her projected form, it was just an eye's blink before she was in Imperial City and flying into the Imperial Palace.

She knew her body was elsewhere, that she was helpless when she performed her sorcery, but it was worth it to calm Publius' worries.

And there he was, in the hallway, for once alone.

He seemed deep in thought, perturbed.

And at that moment she made herself known, allowing his

eyes to see her in her projected form.

"Publius," she said, and though his appearance was as one through a muddled water, she could see his eyes light up, first in surprise, then in happiness, then in anger.

"Julia," Publius said. "I have been worried."

In the shifting vision of her projected form, the hallway which she recognized as the Themis Corridor seemed in motion. But when she focused on Publius, she felt anchored. When she focused on Publius, she could remain in one place.

Father had tried to find her a tutor for her powers, but there were none to be had, for no one could be found that knew the art of projection.

"Julia," Publius said. "How could you do this to me?"

"I will return in time, my love," Julia said.

Not long ago, Publius had been a common man and a humble legionary, a recent recruit. And though it was not forbidden to marry beneath one's station, for the Augusts intermarriage was discouraged, especially for a woman, who assumed her husband's class.

But Publius was August now, the first act of ennoblement by the Imperial Council in many decades. It had been a desperate time.

"But I must warn you… a monster is in Eioli, lying in wait," Julia said. "Human weapons will not harm him. The gods are holding him back, but with each foul sacrifice his despair and anger grows."

She had become convinced the rumors were true, the foul rumors about the Ugars which she had once chalked up to slander. And that was what the Ugars worshiped, the monster in the city, yearning, striving, clawing in his prison.

But if Publius was appreciative of her advice, he showed no sign. He furrowed his brow. "Julia," he said, "you must come back. The Imperial Palace is a nest of vipers. There is talk that the Council is angry, that they will try to remove me."

Remove Publius? It was an outrage. But if a councilor made a motion and there was no objection—if it was unanimous—there was nothing the emperor could do.

She could only imagine why they'd try this.

And it was then that she decided to return to the City. It was then she decided she would face her fears. Publius needed her aid, and she would give it.

Chapter Nine

Aulus Meridius, Centurion

Underneath the slanted shade of stone pines, across fields and hills in the blustery wind and driving rain, Aulus Meridius led the Red Century. They were navigating foreign ground, but their guide, an Ugar traitor, seemed to know the exact path to take.

Aulus was not a fool; he knew what they were doing was extraordinarily risky. There were Ugar patrols about, from Tikal and Hoda and elsewhere, and scouts in abundance. And if the Ugars captured them alive, Aulus could only imagine the horrid things they'd do. They practiced the sacrificing of humans; if they could stoop to that low, they could do anything.

And so as Aulus traversed up and down these brazen hills, past farm fields that the Imperial legion had set alight, he found himself looking this way and that in fear that he would see the enemy.

It seemed to Aulus, as they hurried on, that the Ugars did not favor congregating in small villages, but only in their large cities. He knew there were bears and wildcats about, but perhaps what they feared most was internecine warfare, war between the cities of Tikal and Hoda or between Hoda and Eioli. They cowered behind their walls and would not leave their safety.

The chill was fading as he walked, the rain and the clouds opening up to let in sunlight. The air was crisp and there were signs of life—green coloring—amid the gold hills.

It was high noon when they stopped. "Devil's Dolmen," as it was called, was said to be no more than two days away. The Ugar traitor, if he was to be believed, would lead them there along the least traveled route.

They gathered around and began to eat quietly, snacking on the waybread and drinking the water they had brought in waterskins, and as he ate the tasteless morsels Aulus Meridius began to wonder, and to question everything.

The grand legate Hastatus had told them to go to Devil's Dolmen and nothing else, saying that it would be obvious what he wanted when he got there. And what sort of name was Devil's Dolmen?

He knew one people group of the peninsula, the Cymbri, related to neither the Geats nor the Ugars, were known to build monoliths of stone called dolmens. It was they who worshiped the god of the underworld, Yblis, and built shrines to him in the black spaces beneath the Hollow Hills.

And so as his subordinates ate, he pulled the Ugar traitor aside. The Ugar was thin, and ribs were showing where his tunic did not cover. He was not eating; it seemed he did not want to.

"What," Aulus said, "is Devil's Dolmen?" He spoke at what was almost a whisper.

"That is what others call it," the Ugar traitor said. "And your lord Hastatus has told me not to tell anyone what it is, any soldier, least of all you. That is my oath…"

But the Ugars were oath breakers.

Aulus Meridius could press him but he would not. An order from Hastatus was an order from the grand legate. Aulus would ask no more.

~

In the night time the land was dark, and only the moon and stars gave light.

Aulus felt as if he were in a dream, or in a nightmare. The noises of the screech owls and the night birds formed an uncanny melody. And he realized he was afraid, not just of the Ugars, but of the land itself, the land he was now in.

Chapter Ten

Emperor Publius Corvus

Publius Corvus, emperor. He had had no time to think on it, how absurd the notion was, how far fetched. He had busied himself so much with the preparation of war and the conniving of the councilors, he hadn't a spare breath.

But as he stood on the Great Porch, looking over the city, he did find a spare moment. He realized he still could not believe it, he could not conceive of or understand what had happened to him. The weeks seemed to have melded into one long day. From dawn until late in the night he was with this or that magister, plotting the war or receiving the entreaties of ambassadors and foreign kings. Yet what he had thought about most in that time was Julia. Now he knew she was safe.

And at that thought, he found himself able to exhale a little bit, able to breathe.

But there was a shout.

The Legis was standing at the doorway, dressed in his outdated leather armor. "You are summoned to the Council House, Signor Emperor."

Publius ground his teeth at the thought. But a legal summons was not wisely ignored. In spare moments, he had tried to learn the law. He learned the powers that the Council had, but not much on how to thwart them.

"Very well," Publius said. "I may be a moment."

He would make them wait and imagine seeing them squirm. They had made his life difficult. They could afford to sit a while. And so he stood there, imagining, as the sun rose over the city below. He waited, and under his breath, he prayed.

There was a presence behind him, one he recognized, one he could not forget.

And as he turned and saw Julia's face, her blonde hair, her blue eyes, her luscious lips, he met her in an embrace.

"Julia," was all he could afford to say.

The hem of her gown was stained with mud. Clearly, she had been roughing it.

"The Imperial Council has summoned me," Publius said.

Julia's eyes narrowed. "I will be with you, then, my love."

~

The Council House was as august as the councilors sitting on its benches.

Built of white marble, it seemed to fluoresce in the light of the oculus many fathoms above.

Yet for all its grandeur, Publius had come to hate this place.

And when the councilors saw Julia tagging along, she was met with hisses and jeers.

"Julia!" snapped the Speaker Lychicus. "You were not summoned.

"And you are no longer the emperor's daughter. There is no royal family in the Empire. There is no such thing as a princess in the Empire, though you may have caused people to think it."

"You're right, Lychicus!" Julia said. "I am not the emperor's daughter. But soon I will be the emperor's wife."

Had she seen the ring he had bought her?

"And so I will take my place on the Yellow Seat," Julia said. "If you object, you'll have to send soldiers to pry me out."

The Yellow Seat, next to the White Seat, belonged to the emperor's wife or female relative. Publius smiled as he saw Julia, so cross and so wonderfully insolent, take her seat with a loud harrumph.

"Dress better, then," Lychicus continued. "Show some respect."

Her clothes were tattered, but Julia didn't seem to care. "I only show respect to those who deserve it, Lychicus," she said.

There was redness on Lychicus' cheeks now, and his eyes blazed with wrath.

The Legis entered from the outer door.

"Men of the Council," Lychicus said. "*Numera!*"

How Publius hated that word.

One, two, the Legis counted. Eventually he ended. All twenty-nine councilors were here, all save Agatho Lornodoris, whose death had led to an empty seat in Harbor District.

"Signor Emperor," Lychicus said with acid in his tone, "Evidence has become known to the Council that your nomination was fraudulent."

"Fraudulent," Publius scoffed. "I did not ask for this, Signor Speaker, but this position was given to me. And I will take it."

"Silence," Lychicus said. "There will be order in this house.

"Your name was found by the consultancy of augurs. And we have reason to believe that the augur who cast the die and nominated you was no augur at all, but a skilled imitator installed by shadowy forces."

"Shadowy forces?" Publius said. "What shadowy forces?"

The clerk was nowhere to be seen; this session of the Council appeared to be off-record.

But as for shadowy forces, he could not help but remember the men dressed in black who had been following him in Villa Fort, who had led him to Julia.

And then he wondered if his position was no accident or act from above after all.

"Shadowy forces that remain to be determined," Lychicus said. "Shadowy forces that we will soon uncover. And if there is criminal intent behind it, impostor, we will see you hauled before a judge."

"Objection!" Julia rose from her seat. "Insulting the emperor…"

"You are not a member of the Council," Lychicus hissed. "Another word and I will have you ordered out.

"No objection has been made. This body stands united. And though we find our nation in a moment of peril, the rule of law is the most important thing of all. And so I make a motion to dismiss this impostor from his position as emperor."

There were a few moments of silence; Publius began to panic. No councilor raised his hand or said anything.

Was it all over?

Then Julia stood up. "Publius!" she cried. "Take your seat."

And so he ran over to the White Seat and sat upon it.

Julia laughed openly. "I know your arcane rules," she said. "While the emperor sits, you may not dismiss him."

"Until the convening of the Council ends," Lychicus was smiling, "at dawn two days from now, or until the emperor leaves his place."

"I will feed him and bring him water," Julia said.

"Very well," Lychicus said. "A delay of two days, and this impostor will be dismissed. And you may bring on yourself criminal liability, Julia, if you had any hand in installing the augur."

"Bring all your laws and swords on me, Lychicus," Julia said. "I am not afraid of you. I have seen it all."

Publius was lucky to have Julia, for many reasons. She knew the arcane rules of the Council; she knew the way the Council operated. Perhaps, her father had thwarted these thirty doddering old men before.

And so he sat and he smiled as he watched Lychicus and the others squirm.

Two days, he realized. He had two days to stop this, two

days to convince a councilor or find some other, more obscure rule to invoke.

Chapter Eleven

Marcus Corvus

What was he getting into?

As he stood there at the edge of the crowd in Lorenus Square, he realized he wasn't sure. But thus far he had exulted in every moment, in the times where he had not been stricken with a strange panic or fallen ill.

Lorenus Square overlooked the sea. There were two speeches before the people voted tomorrow.

And Spurius Arappo was there, chattering on as he made grand gestures. The people of Harbor District looked bored.

"And my opponent, one Marcus Corvus—who has heard of him?—has no illustrious family history. The Arappo clan was there in the founding, in the Empire's early days. Will you place your ward under the command of one of little note and scarce nobility?"

Yet Marcus sensed Arappo's words were not penetrating the crowd, that they did not care, that those who had attended either had nothing else to do or were here out of some misguided sense of duty.

"My opponent—" His voice was changed, it was raspy and lion-like, animalistic, like a roar—"wants to send you to die in war. He wants to spill your blood, to put the interests of the Empire's allies second to your own."

Marcus backed away a moment but it was as if the crowd had not noticed the strangeness of the voice.

Some of their ears had perked up and there was grumbling.

War, the spilling of blood, the interests of the Empire or its allies… where had Arappo gotten the notion?

And the air seemed changed, and Marcus' heart began to

flutter.

He wondered what was going on.

But Arappo was leaving the lectern. It was Marcus' turn to make his case.

And so, stunned and confused, wondering what had gone on, he moved to the lectern, climbing the platform, slightly rattled, seeing the faces in the crowd had somewhat turned against him.

"I confess I am no noble," Marcus Corvus said. "My ennoblement was only a happy accident. But because I was once common, because I was once like the majority of you, I will fight for you all the more, because I remember where I came from."

The angry faces seemed to have diminished in number, but still there was something palpable in the air, tension and fear.

And among the crowd he noticed there were a few men garbed in black, and in the front one with the symbol of an eye on his necklace.

"You will know I am one of you when you see the laws I pass," Marcus continued. "I will ensure the fair treatment of the city poor. I will ensure your streets are clean, that justice is done to thieves and robbers…"

His speech was not as effective as he had hoped. But he still believed he could win—it might take a miracle, but he could win.

"I propose a new deepening of the harbor, a refurbishing of the Temple of Lorenus…"

The temple of the sea god, built on a high hill in the middle of the district, was considered a wonder of the world.

"And moreover, I will ensure the wars with the Ugars are brought to a quick, safe, and victorious end."

There was a change in the air, the fear pulsing brighter than ever, and Marcus strained to catch his breath. But he steeled himself; he looked out to the crowd, and saw them begin to disperse.

It was then, for the first time, that he thought he was going to lose.

Chapter Twelve

Emperor Publius Corvus

It was dark and the Council had long departed. There was no illumination except the moon.

Julia had left him alone in the Council chamber, and per her orders he remained in the White Seat. This delaying tactic would work for another day. Then, who knew?

Julia was gone to the Conciliar Library, hoping to find some rule to invoke, some way to overcome the conniving of the councilors.

And the situation had caused him to think, for better or worse, to remember the strange incidents that had popped up in the days before he'd become emperor.

The black-garbed agents had led him to Julia. The black-garbed agents had restrained Maria Domina, a sorceress of great power who might well have been a match for Publius.

But no, no, there was no deception in his actions, no scheming. If the augury was a forgery, he'd had no part in it.

In the almost total darkness he barely made out a shape moving toward him. It was coming from the Sky Bridge.

There was a spark; a wick was lit. A lamp began to glow.

It was Julia, and judging by the expression on her face, it would seem that she had failed.

"Books, books, books," Julia said.

She had been gone from his side for hours and he had missed her.

"I know the words are in Imperial," Julia said, "but they are in a strange dialect. What would you call it? Legalite. I do not understand hardly a word."

"And so what do we do, my love?" Publius said.

"I will try to convince a councilor," Julia said.

"And if you don't?" Publius said.

Julia was silent. She leaned over to him, kissed him. "Every day is troubling enough," she said. "Let's not think on the worst until it happens."

The worst. Was losing his position the worst, or would the councilors not be satisfied? Would they go after him?

Thoughts continued to percolate. At times he felt as dark as this room, lit only by the scant light of Julia's hope. And he said, "What happened? The augur, a skilled imitator… Is it true? Am I a fraud?"

"You are no fraud," Julia said, "regardless of what happened."

Sometimes, Publius wondered if Julia knew more than she let on.

"You are where you are meant to be, on the White Throne," Julia said. "You are where the gods want you to be."

Her trite words did not comfort him. No, they did not.

He was full of fear, full of worry. Sleeping in this seat would not be easy. There were no councilors and the Council Guard had long left the chambers. He wondered if anyone would see him slip away, but it was best not to take a risk.

"We will beat this," Publius said. "Some way, somehow, we will beat this. And I can't wait to see the look on Lychicus' face when we do."

Chapter Thirteen

Marcus Corvus

The sun rose on the day of Marcus' destiny.

His sleep had been weak and brief; he had struggled all night and managed probably less than an hour. But he awoke alert, anxious, even afraid.

And as the light peeked in through Flavia and Demetrius' windows, he knew—whatever happened—it would be a day he would remember for the rest of his life, a day his hopes were realized or a day his hopes were dashed and scattered to pieces on the floor.

He put on his finest tunic, a bright thing of scarlet, and his finest breeches, colored a dark black. He laid over his neck the necklace of false diamonds he'd purchased a little while back. He was an August by law; he needed to seem one by rights.

He looked at himself in the drawing room mirror.

And as he looked at himself, he met his own gaze.

He sensed a presence behind him.

And a voice he thought he heard: "You will not win." The voice was deep, but he was not sure if he had just imagined it.

And the glassy surface of the mirror seemed to have fogged up.

"I will win," Marcus said to whoever he had heard, even if it were his own mind. "I will win, and you will watch me win."

~

The skies were blue and clear. Voting was under way in Lorenus Square.

The rabble of Harbor District were casting their votes, their choices marked on potsherds. Every free male of the city, who owned some small bit of property and lived in a dwelling, was allowed to vote. And vote they would, whether it was for Spurius Arappo or for Marcus Corvus.

As Marcus Corvus watched them cast their potsherds before the ward magistrates, he found himself wondering if he could have done better, if he could have made himself more known, if he could have made more generous and even more unfeasible promises.

But one could always look back on the past and adjust. One could always do something better, after the fact.

In all he had done what he could; he had done his best. And now he watched the results with trepidation. He anticipated failure.

Voting ended at the ninth hour. Then there would be a period of counting. He would be there to face the result, whatever it was.

He was not the praying type, but he uttered under his breath, "Gods above, good gods, please let me be the victor."

Though he scanned Lorenus Square, he could not see Spurius Arappo. How haughty was he, so sure of the result that he would not bother attending.

Hundreds upon hundreds, thousands upon thousands, were casting their potsherds into pots.

It was a strange thing, voting, choosing your leaders. What would the barbarians of the north, with their chiefs and clans think?

Chapter Fourteen

Emperor Publius Corvus

By virtue of his sitting in the White Seat, no conciliar business could be conducted.

And so he was there alone amid the Council chamber's majestic marble facades and arches. The skies had cleared up and the sun was shining down in the oculus. The weather was warmer and there was a taste of spring in the air.

Publius had grown sore in the seat. It wasn't meant for relaxing. He had struggled to sleep all night but had eventually found an uncomfortable position to sleep in.

What strange things were the rules of the Council, how odd and illogical that its processes could hamper the passing of laws. And they all seemed to revere these strange rules and "precedents," and would never dare to break them.

Julia was walking in from the Sky Bridge. She was like a figure wreathed in light, standing outside.

Her cheeks were red; there was a slightly angry expression on her face.

Clearly, she had failed.

"They will not listen to reason," she said when she'd gotten within hearing distance. And she collapsed, weeping, on his knees.

Now it was Publius who had to be confident; it was Publius who had to comfort her.

"Oh, Publius, what will happen to us?" Julia said. "What will happen to us?"

"We will beat this," Publius said. "We will beat this. Just watch."

No councilors could be convinced, and whether Publius was confident or not he did not truly know. But he had a feeling he'd emerge the victor. He had a feeling he'd remain emperor for a long time.

Chapter Fifteen

Marcus Corvus

Failure.

Failure!

"The votes being counted," the ward legate announced before the scattered crowds, "are fifteen thousand to five thousand. The people have chosen Spurius Arappo as their champion."

Marcus felt like a pile of stones had fallen on him, first shock, then denial, then shame… deep, deep shame.

Who had he thought he was? Who had he believed himself to be?

How could he have ever imagined becoming a councilor was possible?

What a failure Marcus Corvus had turned out to be.

Chapter Sixteen

Emperor Publius Corvus

Why, where, and how had it gotten to this point?

Julia was asleep on the floor, at his feet.

It was dark, almost pitch black. He had gotten sore.

His confidence had begun to fade. Dawn was coming, and with it, the opportunities of this strange legal maneuver would vanish into the sun.

And then what? Emperor Publius would be emperor no more.

Perhaps, that was what should be.

But he, too, was curious about who the "augur" was, and why—of all people—he had been interested in Publius.

It was dark, deeply dark, and he was sore.

But there was noise rising above the gentle wind, and in the distance, through the doorway, on the Sky Bridge, a person was approaching. He was carrying a lantern.

For a moment, his hopes arose, and he imagined it was Lychicus offering an olive branch.

But this person's gait was young, nimble, athletic, even sprightly. And as he drew closer, he saw it was not Lychicus, nor any councilor he recognized.

He was wearing dark clothing, and had a dark hood over his head. His eyes were gleaming in the lanternlight.

"Who are you?" said Publius.

Finally, he was just inches from Publius, and just inches from Julia, sleeping on the floor.

"I," said the man, "am Sextus, and you owe everything you have to me."

He saw that over the man's neck a necklace was draped, of

gold chain, with an eye insignia in the center.

Interlude I

The emperor did not understand everything the agent of the Empire told him, nor—after the end of his words—why he of all citizens had been chosen.

But worse were the agent's plans, plans that could help the emperor and the Empire but were of questionable goodness, plans that would lead to violence and possible unrest.

Chapter Seventeen

The sun had not yet arisen when there was a knock on the door.

Marcus Corvus jerked up from his divan. His sleep had been interrupted.

He had come to terms with his failure; he had come to terms with losing the councillorship. Flavia and Demetrius had comforted him in his distress.

There was knocking again, louder this time, and a faint shout.

And so Marcus hurriedly donned his clothes.

He walked to the front door of Flavia and Demetrius' house and opened it, seeing that the ward legate of Harbor District was there.

Behind him were men of the urban cohorts, dressed in armor, with swords and shields at the ready.

Had they come to arrest him?

"What is this?" said Marcus.

"Spurius Arappo took violently ill and died last night," said the ward legate. "By law, you are Harbor District's new councilor. In the end, you were the people's only option."

Marcus' reaction was not joy. Instead, he was concerned. What a strange turn of events had occurred, and what a golden opportunity had fallen into his lap.

And he did not know what to say. And so he only stared, and wondered, and questioned.

Chapter Eighteen

Emperor Publius Corvus

"A motion is made." Speaker Lychicus was in the Council's August halls.

Publius was in the White Seat with a smile on his face.

"I move that this emperor, this impostor, be dismissed," said Lychicus.

And for a little while there was silence. In the Yellow Seat, Julia sat, positively gloating.

For a moment, Publius wondered if his brother too had turned against him.

But no; the councilor from Harbor District, Marcus Corvus, stepped forward. "I object," Marcus said, and the motion was defeated.

Publius would remain emperor. He and Julia had emerged the victors.

Chapter Nineteen

Aulus Meridius, Centurion

The Red Century reached Devil's Dolmen later than they had hoped, on the third day, at dusk.

What was called the Devil's Dolmen was set upon a high hill, the highest hill for miles around.

It was a statue of the Ugars' god, Belpheor.

The statue was of bronze, a beastly thing with a bull's head and the body of a man, its hands formed in a cupped position.

And in the light of dusk, Aulus Meridius, leader of the Red Century, found himself appalled.

Stone pines were like crooked shadows in the distance. Here, on the high hill, one could see for miles around.

"What is this?" Aulus said. "What is this?"

Their guide, the Ugar traitor, walked before the great bronze statue of Belpheor.

"Now," said the Ugar traitor, "it is my turn to lead. Somewhere here there is stored wood and coal. We shall make it heat up."

The guide's words were as good as a command from Hastatus. The Red Century began to disperse, searching for the storehouse, but Aulus could not bring himself to move.

He had a feeling he knew what was coming.

Would Hastatus, the grand legate overseeing the siege of Eioli, really stoop this low? Did he really believe the Ugars' god had any potency?

Aulus Meridius had witnessed plagues and visitations of dark spirits. If the Empire used such powers against their enemies, they were no better than the Ugars.

But the Red Century found the storehouse of wood and

coal, in a trapdoor on the ground. They began to pile the wood in a cavity within the statue. And Aulus, following the orders of Hastatus and Hastatus alone, trying to convince himself that he was doing his duty, joined in.

~

By the time night fell, the fire was raging, and the statue of Belpheor had grown so hot it glowed a bright red.

"Now," the Ugar traitor said, "we shall invoke his aid."

He was holding two binds.

And Aulus Meridius was suddenly unwilling to go any further. He was unwilling to do this. He was unwilling to act.

"No Imperial shall be sacrificed," Aulus said. It was a firm order, and he did not care if he was disobeying the grand legate. Such barbaric customs could never be followed.

"Not an Imperial," said the Ugar traitor. "Me."

"You," Aulus said, appalled all the more. He wanted no part of this. He would have no part of this.

He had been faithful to his oath, even invoking the gods in the Rite of Devotion. He had been faithful to his oath, obeying his commander in everything.

But he could not do this, no, he could not.

"If you will not," cried his lieutenant Nivus, "then I will."

And Aulus watched, appalled as he had ever been, as his lieutenant—a burly giant of a man—strode forth and crudely jerked a hold of the Ugar traitor.

And up the wooden steps he walked, and though the Ugar traitor came willingly his lieutenant was twisting him this way and that.

Aulus stepped back. Disgust was molting into fear. He felt the eyes of that wicked statue watching him.

And then he heard a desperate cry as his lieutenant cast the

Ugar traitor down, down, down, onto the bronze hands, where his body quickly began to burn up.

~

Sores blazed into existence on Nivus' arms and legs, bright red sores. His eyes burst and they began to bleed.

But though he was bleeding, racked with pestilence, he was laughing, yes, he was laughing…. A deep cackle.

The air seemed to have changed; winds were twisting all about Aulus, evil winds.

The men of the Red Century were looking this way and that in confusion. And Aulus, having washed his hands of this, was backing away.

The statues' glow seemed to be growing.

There was a loud cry; a legionary ran up to Aulus. Sores had appeared on him too, sores that were bleeding. He began to cough up blood.

There were other cries, and more pestilence was appearing.

Aulus, disgusted, turned and ran, leaving his century behind him.

But he had not gotten a yard away from them when he was stopped.

A beast was there, and its eyes were glowing yellow in the darkness. If a bull, it was the largest of all bulls. Fumes were emerging from its breath.

"Bulls," Aulus found himself saying. "Great Bulls of Phaegor!"

Part Two

Chapter Twenty

Julia Seánus

Julia jerked awake.

It was the middle of the night, but she was lathed in a cold sweat.

She felt as if something terrible had just happened, something terrible, something far away but that was close to her heart.

Close to my heart…

Publius, she thought, but she quickly realized that wasn't it.

No, her heart was trembling, and she sensed the world was in peril.

What had happened?

With fear, she remembered the monster of Eioli, the monster yearning to break free.

Her bedchamber was almost pitch dark. It was spare; it had not been refurbished.

"Publius," she said aloud, this time.

Perhaps, it was him after all. Perhaps, she sensed he was in danger.

And so she hurriedly changed from her smallclothes into a light smock, something she could bear being seen in.

And fighting panic, she fled out, down the winding corridors of the Imperial Palace. At a corner, one of the Imperial Guards was napping… that built her confidence, surely.

When she reached the Imperial bedchamber, she sped past the guards without a word.

Publius lay in his bed, fast asleep.

He was doing well, protected by a single objection of his brother. All was well for him. All was well.

So why was she so troubled?

As if in answer, Publius jerked awake, gasping for air like a fish out of water.

His eyes were glassy and wide.

"Publius," Julia said.

He looked at her. "I've had a bad dream, I think," he said, "but I can't remember a whit of it."

Julia walked closer to him, sat on his bed though it was against the decorum of the Imperial Palace.

"And I couldn't sleep either," Julia said.

Publius seemed to have calmed down.

"Care," said she, "to go on a journey?"

Publius, winking his eyes, laid a hold of her hands. They had only done this a few times before.

~

When she brought another with her in her projected state, it was all the more tiring, all the more difficult. She'd surely wake up exhausted and bereft of energy.

But she was carrying Publius away. He was a faint form, a dark shadow, and when she sojourned with him his vision was dark and dim, like a foggy glass.

But carry him she did, and they zipped out of the Imperial Palace, above the buildings, and soon the urban and suburban sprawl was behind them.

Across villages and hamlets they traveled, underneath the moon and stars, in the dead of night, and as she turned north-westwards she could not help but feel her growing dread.

In a land of dark rich silt, in a land crowned with stone pines and darkly-flowered bushes, she saw in fear a blazing statue, a statue so hot it had turned red. Beside it bodies lay.

Far ahead was a dark figure riding on a bull.

"What is this?" Publius said, and Julia wondered what he could see. "What is this?"

A voice bellowed. The statue's mouth moved. "I have won." Deep was the voice, raspy like that of a lion. It was almost a roar. "The Empire is mine…"

And Julia fell back, soaring away as if driven by a wind.

Publius followed a moment later, falling backward, soaring to where his body was.

They were back in his bedroom, back in their bodies, not in their projected state.

And if there was fear on Publius' face he showed no sign of it. He seemed to have hardened with resolve. "Julia," said he, "there are urgent matters. We must ensure Eioli's fall."

Chapter Twenty-One

Aulus Meridius, Centurion

"Bulls," said Aulus, "Great Bulls of Phaegor!"

The metallic beast was hurtling through the fields. Other beasts had joined him; it was like a stampede in the grasslands of Khandara.

The dawn's light was twinkling over the hills. The Bull of Phaegor would not let Aulus fall.

And Aulus knew he could not escape.

The Bull of Phaegor was almost flying, he was so speedy.

And overhead, clouds had begun to gather. In his heart, Aulus sensed the coming doom.

Over the hills they bounded.

The city appeared in the horizon, the legions and the fortifications that surrounded them. In a span of hours the bulls had finished a journey that took the Red Century three days.

Crash went the palisades. The Bulls of Phaegor trampled the legionaries underfoot, and at last they reached the gate.

Aulus was bucked off the bull's back and he went flying.

Their horns struck the gate of Eioli, and the gate of Eioli fell with a great crash.

Chapter Twenty-Two

Aulus Meridius, Centurion

Aulus was limping when he arose. The defenders of Eioli had massed amid the rubble of the gate.

He drew his sword.

If there was love for the Empire in his heart, he no longer felt it. If there was hatred for Eioli in his heart, he had seen what a fellow Imperial had done.

He looked about and saw the Imperials eager, as if thirsty for blood. He could see them as if they had horns on their heads, as if they were beasts and not human beings.

What foul order had Aulus obeyed? What had he done? What, indeed, had he done?

Chapter Twenty-Three

Emperor Publius Corvus

The wedding ceremony was a quiet affair.

In the Imperial Palace, before the Great Porch, he peered into Julia's eyes. She was as beautiful as she had been when she appeared to him in the snow all those months ago.

She was in a white gown; she had removed her veil.

The priest of Imperium, the Spirit of Empire, was leading them in their vows.

And of Publius' family, Marcus was here, and Flavia and Demetrius as well… but Marcella was gone and he did not know why. She had been invited.

Lychicus was here; he seemed to have gained a new respect for Publius for thwarting him, but the investigations went on and Publius was not altogether safe.

"Julia Seánus, daughter of Marcus Seánus and Ulpia Ajax, your parents are not here to see you off," the priest said. "But I am confident they would approve of a man of such mettle."

Where, indeed, was Julia's family? Her parents were gone, but no relatives were present and among those seated were only her old friends, the same age as she.

"Publius Corvus, you are of new blood," said the priest. "And Julia is of old. But this is a wedding of equals, for August are you both."

Publius did not know why he needed to mention it.

He was peering into Julia's eyes, and he could tell something was bothering her.

The wedding had happened so quickly. But Publius had seen that look in her eyes before, and he knew it was not him, it was not this. Her mind, as always, was elsewhere, always focused on the great things and not the petty, the things that mattered in the larger sense.

"We come gathered today to celebrate the union of our new emperor and empress," the priest was droning on and Publius had begun to lose focus.

He would remember this day for the rest of his life, yes, and when he was old and gray, but still he was thinking on what he had seen, on the statue, on the city of Eioli which had so often slipped from the Empire's grasp.

Eioli… something terrible was at work there.

Publius looked back. There were so many empty seats in this makeshift chapel, set up quickly on the Great Porch. The city lay before them, stretching into the distance, and the dark blue waters of the sea.

Eioli… all he could think about was Eioli.

But he looked once again at Julia. How fortunate he was to have her. How fortunate, indeed, was he to be where he was.

"And so I ask…" The priest of Imperium's words had become background noise, hard to distinguish, but his question sharpened Publius into focus. "Publius Corvus, formerly of Seafarers' Way, do you take Julia Seánus, formerly of Kings Street and Myrtle Row, as your wife?"

"I do," Publius said, and some of those worries about larger things faded.

A bit of the worry seemed to have drained from Julia's face as well, but not all.

"Julia Seánus, formerly of Kings Street and Myrtle Row, do you take Publius Corvus as your husband?"

"I do," said Julia.

And it was done. The two of them were wed.

~

The feast that night was more sparsely attended than the wedding.

Lychicus and certain other magisters had let Publius and Julia alone.

But such a feast Publius had never seen, with roast quail rubbed with spice and turnips in the style of the Ugars. Such a feast Publius had never seen, before or since, in his time as a soldier or as the emperor. Four courses were served, quail and turnips followed by haunches of beef and great rashers of bacon, swordfish and dolphinfish, pies stuffed with meat and laden with cream, followed by sweetbreads and puddings and jellies, and then finally roasted greens. Each course was served with as much wine as any guest wanted, and by the end of it the table was filthy, splashed red, and bones were scattered on the floor.

Yet Julia, for all the grandeur, seemed to talk less and less as the night wore on, though Publius knew she loved him.

"Where are you honeymooning?" said Marcus Corvus, Publius' brother and new councilor. He had drunk the most wine of all.

"Eioli," Julia said, and there were gasps among her gathered friends. "We are honeymooning in Eioli."

~

After the ecstasy of the night, Julia lay in bed next to Publius, scarcely clothed.

She ran a finger over the length of his chin.

"Empress Julia Seánus," she said. "I rather like the name."

"Julia Corvus," Publius said. "You are a Corvus now."

"Indeed," Julia said. "I suppose I am. I rather like it that way."

But though she was happy, Publius could tell something was bothering her beneath the surface.

"Julia Corvus," Julia was whispering. "Julia Seánus Corvus. The name Ajax slips further and further away..."

Though he and Julia were wed, though he loved her, though they had become one, still he felt there were things he didn't know about her, things he didn't understand or didn't think to question. The more he knew, the more chambers were opened, the more hidden compartments, the more secret rooms. But he supposed, by the end of his life, he would know all there was to know about Julia Seánus.

"Julia Seánus Corvus," she said at a whisper. She was drifting off to sleep.

Publius touched her hand. His bedchamber was dark and dim.

"I think something is on Julia Seánus Corvus' mind," Publius said.

Her eyes were shut. She had fallen limp.

"Eioli." It was an answer from the heart. "Eioli... Belpheor..."

Chapter Twenty-Four

Aulus Meridius, Legionary

With each thundering boom of a falling stone, the catapults reminded the men of the Sixth Anthanian they were behind them.

Buildings were collapsing; fires had started all over the city. Aulus did not need reminding that the battle was raging far into the night.

The collapse of the gate, and the suddenness of its fall, had lit a fire underneath the men of the Imperial legions. It was a great shift in the momentum, a great shift in the feeling of battle. It was the onslaught of hope.

But as Aulus fought the Ugars with his brothers, slashing with his sword, trying to break beyond the rubble of the gate, he realized the fire that had been lit scared him, and the eagerness with which the Imperial fought was uncanny. Indeed, it seemed unnatural.

He knew what had been done; he knew what he had allowed to occur, what he had not fought with all his might. And as he battled, shield to shield with his brothers, he felt like the only one who was not eager, the only one who did not want to taste blood. And he hoped the gods in heaven would forgive him for what had been done.

There was a loud crash.

He looked up. Against the crescent moon, he saw a spire of Eioli's great temple had been struck by a catapult. The spire fell in a rain of brick and masonry. Ugars wailed in the distance.

The fire rises.

The legionaries fought more furiously than ever. Though it was night, it seemed more and more of their swords were striking home, and the Ugars would not be able to beat them back.

The stars were bright pinpoints of light against a dark mantle.

Boom!—another boulder fell, another building collapsed, another structure caught flame.

But as Aulus drove forward, he realized how little progress they had made. All the people of the city—every Ugar, man and woman—had joined to block their entrance.

It was late at night, perhaps midnight, when the orders came… to back off, retreat, and to wait until day.

Chapter Twenty-Five

Empress Julia

The sun rose on the morning after their wedding.

It was their first day as man and wife, the first full day she would have as empress.

And yet, in the great wardrobe, as she picked out her gown, she realized just how much there was to do, just how much there was left undone.

Publius did not know all about her; he did not know everything, not yet.

In the end she picked the perfect attire: a great billowing thing of gold-and-silver tissue. Over her legs she would wear hose, and she would have white gloves on her hands. On her head she would place a white diadem.

And it struck her, then, that she had become what she had hated in her youth, the pomp, the ceremony, the callous disregard that the upper classes had for the common. She had heard their sneering commentary for the rabble of Imperial City; and she had argued with them, stating that they too were children of the gods, the result of bad luck and nothing more.

But as her servants fitted her into her gown, she realized this was what she was. She was August, an Ajax, a Seánus, a Corvus.

It was who she was meant to be.

~

The servants carried Julia on a litter down the hallway. She intended to go to Harbor District to make some purchases. The best of the clothiers and dress-makers lived there, and jewelers were there as well, jewelers of masterful talent. The public funds for the emperor and empress were technically unlimited and now she could not help but make use of them.

But there was a shout. "Julia!" Through the netted window of the litter she could make out a red-faced Lychicus standing at the doorway.

"You are summoned to a meeting of the Council," he said.

Julia sighed, and removed her veil. "Let me out," she said.

~

In the Council chamber she stood, in her billowing gown of gold-and-silver tissue, her hose and her white gloves, the diadem on her head and the emerald necklace on her neck.

"You have returned to your old ways," said Speaker Lychicus.

Julia could see that Publius was on the White Seat, observing the Council's proceedings. He had arisen before her; he wore only a jet black tunic and russet breeches, a Hieronian holy symbol on his neck and the Silver Circlet on his head. He was a humble man, humbler than she, humbler than she could afford to be.

"Your husband has proposed you both personally oversee the Eioli operation," Lychicus said. "Or are you more interested in dresses of white samite and jeweled chaplets?"

"Don't belittle me, Lychicus." Julia by now was before the Council, and though she was scornful of them they truly were imposing. The rows of councilors were many tiers and stretched up to the ceiling. One almost felt like an ant before them.

But Julia would not be intimidated. She had seen everything, even in her youth when her father spoke, her youth… her youth, she thought, and was full of regret.

She tried to regain her poise. "We are leaving soon," Julia said. "We will personally oversee it. That is my mission. And how dare you criticize, me, Lychicus. I must look well if I am to inspire the troops."

Lychicus sneered, but there was scattered laughter among the councilors seated.

"Agatho Lornodoris tried to personally oversee the Eioli operation," Lychicus said. "Remember him?"

No, she did not remember.

"No, you do not," Lychicus said. "He was murdered by the Ugars. We will not have that happen again.

"And you do not remember, Julia, because you were gone. And now the Council has evidence you were a member of the barbaric Red Hand cult."

"Enough!" Publius shouted and Lychicus seemed to back down.

Yet Julia's crossness, her confidence bordering on pride, evaporated in that moment, and she was a shell of herself, a mouse and not a woman, a mouse and not a human being.

She had forgotten. Why hadn't she thought of it? The Council was always investigating behind the scenes. She would be exposed.

"For reasons of safety," Lychicus said, "and for reasons of your own legal peril, I make a motion to keep the Imperial family here, in the city, and have them observe the war from afar.

"Let the Legis make a vote."

The clerk in the distance got out his quill pen. He had opened his book.

The Legis strode forward, the stupid Legis in his outdated armor, that wretched Legis who threatened to ruin her.

And like that Julia's world fell apart, for she knew the arm of the law was bearing down on her, the arm of the law that neither Corvus nor Ajax could escape.

Chapter Twenty-Six

Emperor Publius Corvus

In a side room, Julia had fallen on to him, weeping.

She was reduced.

The law had passed; they were restricted from leaving the city for a period of ten days. And Marcus Corvus and the handful of other objectors were unable to stop it.

"It will be all right," said Publius.

"It will be all right," said Publius, though he did not know whether he spoke the truth or a lie.

And after the weeping had diminished, he thought it was a good time to ask her.

"Did you commit any crimes, Julia?" Publius said. "Did you not tell me everything?"

"Under pressure," Julia said. "Under pressure I did things I never would have done. By the time I had devoted myself completely to it, I had become afraid of them. I had become afraid of Maria Domina. And so—"

"Just tell me," Publius said, "without excuses."

"No excuses," she said softly. "At first, I was willing. When I saw what they wanted to do, I was unwilling. But by the time I slipped away, I was their captive, and they intended to break me. And they did break me, through all manner of means. I had no choice—"

"Just tell me what you did," Publius said.

He had a feeling he'd forgive her for anything.

"The robbery of the moneychangers," Julia said. "I held them up at knifepoint."

The incident with the moneychangers had been in his daily report. He had paid it no mind, figuring the urban cohorts would get to the bottom of it.

"The funds were meant to help our operations throughout the city," Julia said. "And there were kidnappings I was aware of, but I took no part."

"What else?" Publius demanded.

"Robberies, many robberies," Julia said. "I was with them when they robbed a jeweler, and I distracted a guard while they robbed a goldsmith."

Publius had begun to worry, now. "Oh, Julia," he said softly. At least she had stopped her weeping.

But he did believe that whatever part she played, she had a limited responsibility. She had been under threat; if she had bought in to the Red Dawn nonsense, well, their cruelty to her had broken her.

"Have you murdered anyone?" said Publius.

"No," she said sharply, and looked up, almost indignant. But that indignation softened.

"No," she said again, softly this time, "not unless you include Varro."

Varro. The trial of the former Imperial Guard had been in his daily brief as well. "Did you cast a spell on him?" he said.

"No," Julia said, "I haven't that kind of power. But I did call him. Like I tried to call you."

There was a long pause. The side room was dark. The Council was still deliberating. But Publius already knew what they had to do.

"Julia," said Publius, "you and I belong together. We are leaving the city, with or without the Council's permission."

"And break the law?" said Julia.

"You are not safe here, not after what you've told me," Publius continued. "We leave, tonight, at dusk. I will still have the armies' command and respect; the Council cannot take that from me.

"Let them send the Council Guard after us. We will have the Imperial Guard."

"A war," said Julia, "between the Council House and the Palace… perhaps, that is our only choice."

Chapter Twenty-Seven

Aulus Meridius

The day dawned over Eioli's walls. The Empire's soldiers had not breached them.

The effort had failed yet again. And the only loss was Aulus' belief in his fellow men, his fellow Imperials. No longer did he look upon those walls with hate.

Where had the Bulls of Phaegor gone? They had broken the gate to bits, and then vanished into the darkness. They were like ghosts or phantoms, here one moment and then vanishing into the air.

And whatever help they brought, Aulus did not want. Only the gods' help he wanted now, and the help of his own hands, his own strength.

The people of Eioli, overnight, had built ramshackle fortifications, nailed together barriers of wood. But it was not as strong as the gate, and with effort the Imperials could break toward them once more.

Horns echoed, a series of horns.

Aulus turned.

In the distance, he could see that Eioli's reinforcements had arrived, a great army that stretched into the horizon, riding on horses.

They had come to rescue their sister, Eioli… the Ugars of Tikal and Hoda and other cities were here, just as Aulus had feared.

Hastatus in the distance began barking orders. Centuries began to marshal together.

The cities of this dark coast were of one blood. They all had broken their bonds, their friendship with the Empire.

And in this case, the Empire was outnumbered.

The horses fell upon them suddenly, but the Empire's fortifications held firm. Now the legion was pinned between the city of Eioli on one side and its allies on the other. But they fought, and they struggled.

The daylight began to wane. The afternoon shadows grew long, and the shadows of the stone pine seemed stretched. The sally had failed. Once again, the Empire remained in control. The fortifications were enough, and the allies of Eioli began to retreat.

Chapter Twenty-Eight

Empress Julia

Publius—he did not know everything. About her, about her darkest secrets she had told him most of it. But about the Empire and the upper classes and how to survive such a world of cloak and dagger antics he was sorely unprepared.

As she departed with him quietly in the carriage, she knew how harebrained his plans were, to evade the capture of the Council. But even Julia knew it was the best option available to them, albeit one fraught with risk.

The Council Guard was well armed. The Imperial Guard might not go along with it.

But under cover of dusk the carriage was leaving the Imperial Palace stables. Under the cover of dusk they would make their escape.

She peered into Publius' eyes.

"Publius," said she, "before we go... may we make one stop?"

He agreed, but her request would not serve the mission. No, it was the request of one doomed, of one who wanted to enjoy one last pleasure before she met her death.

~

It was not yet night when they reached Harbor District.

The clothier she loved did not close up shop until night.

And Publius was clearly annoyed with her when she exited the carriage. She would try her best not to keep him long.

Brocades and satins, embroideries and jeweled chaplets, all

was available to her, and she purchased them with abandon. There were gowns and dresses of all sizes.

It was her guilty pleasure.

Publius was sacrificing himself for her. None of those crimes she had committed were his. She was lucky to have him.

It was like a visit to the graveyard, this trip, this short detour. She bought a billowing gown of satin, a white smock crafted of silk, a thin tunic encrusted with diamonds. She bought chaplets of yellow, green and white, some embedded with false flowers and others gleaming with ruby.

The price would make even Mother blush, rest her soul.

And then she exited with her bags of things, chest loads of clothing she ought to feel guilty about but didn't.

This, she thought as she passed through the door, *is my last will and testament, Julia Ajax Seánus Corvus.*

The air outside was brisk. The last bits of twilight were fading and the streets were almost dark.

Her husband, Publius, was outside the carriage.

He was talking to a man in black.

He was talking to Sextus.

Gods help us all.

Chapter Twenty-Nine

Emperor Publius Corvus

"Stay and fight," Sextus was saying, "or have you already lost faith in us?"

The things Sextus had told him he was sworn to secrecy for, but he knew how deeply embedded the agents of the Empire were, and how intertwined with Imperial history they were. At all historical events, Publius now questioned things and wondered their hand was in them.

"The law forbids me to leave," Publius said.

Julia, he saw, had just emerged from the clothier.

"The law even I cannot overcome," Publius continued. "So I will disobey it. I sit on the White Throne. Their powers are not superior to mine and my brother will never let them remove me.

"I will watch Eioli… I will see it fall."

"It is ill advised." Sextus' voice had quieted. Julia was now within hearing distance.

"You are harassing my husband?" she said.

Members of the Imperial Guard had walked over and were now helping carry the various chests and bags. Yet even they were struggling to get a handle on them.

Sextus seemed insistent. "If I may offer my advice," he said, "you are taking a path even I cannot protect you from. You are going down a road I would not."

"And so what would I do?" Publius said. "How would I get there?"

The Imperial Guards were now loading the chests into the carriage bed.

"You do not need to go to Eioli, not just yet," Sextus said.

He did not know all; he did not know the visions Julia had

had, the visions Julia had told Publius about. He did not know of the monster yearning to break free, and how Julia was convinced that she, and she alone could destroy it.

"Julia is in danger," said Publius. "Perhaps, if we win a victory—"

Julia was observing silently.

"You go down a dangerous road," said Sextus. "One with which I cannot accompany you. Let the legions face Eioli. Let Julia face justice.

"Do not back down; do not retreat."

But his words were meaningless; his warnings were futile.

"We've heard enough," said Julia. "We leave tonight. We leave now."

~

The carriage rattled through the streets. In the darkness, Publius was on edge. Julia had fallen asleep on his chest. Sextus' warnings lingered over him. The night was deep and dark.

On either side of the carriage, members of the Imperial Guard were riding on horses. It would take more than an hour to get out of city bounds, and then the reach of the Council would be evaded.

Then they would be gone; Julia would be safe from the magistrates and the urban cohorts. She would be safe from arrest.

And then what? He did not know. He could not afford to think more than one step ahead. He knew what the punishments would be for Julia once Varro told all.

He was lucky to have her, sleeping in his arms. He was lucky to have her, and he was lucky to be alive.

~

The carriage shook to a halt and Publius gasped, awakening in a moment's span. There was nickering and neighing from the horses and shouts outside.

He set Julia aside. He got up and looked out the window.

They were surrounded. There were men on every side of them, bearing swords and spears. They were of the urban cohorts, the only legion that was allowed to roam inside the city.

Who had sent them? Who had alerted them?

He thought instantly of Sextus.

But Publius was not one to admit defeat. No; if the Council had done this, or Sextus, why, then, he would get his revenge. He would weasel his way out of this. He would emerge victorious.

The door of the carriage opened, and Julia startled awake.

A man in military dress was there in the dim lamplight, a man of the urban cohorts with a sideways crest on his helmet… perhaps a centurion.

"Julia Seánus," said he, "you are charged with robbery, extortion, sorcery and murder."

Murder?

Fear washed over her face, but Julia—the strong old girl—steeled herself instantly. She wouldn't let them see her in pain; she wouldn't give them the satisfaction.

And Publius did not want to let her go, no, he did not, and his heart ached with despair.

"You will be transported to City Prison until the time of your trial," the centurion continued.

Julia spat in his face. "There is a justice higher than man," she said. "And you may not do anything without their permission."

At such moments her piety shone through, the piety that was revered in the founding generations. And in their time together, as man and wife, it had begun to rub off on Publius as well. More so than the Hieronian symbol around his neck, Julia was his guiding light, a candle that led heavenward.

I will see her through this, though in his heart he was unsure. *She will emerge the victor.*

But his heart was trembling, and as she exited the carriage he wondered if it was the last time he'd ever see his wife.

~

"Sextus, Sextus," Publius was uttering before the Great Porch.

Outside, rain was coming down in sheets and thunder had just rumbled.

"Sextus," said Publius, "have you done this? Was your hand in this?"

His wife, the empress, was in City Prison.

He had returned to the Imperial Palace, for he would not leave without her. He was acutely aware of his responsibilities; he was the leader of the nation—a hard fact to believe, even now, one he wasn't sure he believed even as he experienced it.

"A valiant effort." A voice spoke from behind.

Lychicus.

When Publius turned, he was almost at a growl. "Do you know what you've done?"

"I had no part in it, emperor." Lychicus was smiling faintly. "Do you know that Varro's trial is ended? He was sentenced to die by beheading."

Lychicus was holding something in his hands, a necklace with a white gem.

"This, I believe, is your wife's."

"Why did you do this, Lychicus?" Publius said again, insistent.

Lychicus' smile evaporated. "I had no part. Your ploy was clever, more clever than you know. Your disappearance would have raised questions of law, questions the Council is not posed to answer. You were leaving in the dead of night and what could be done?

"But a writ had been issued for your wife's arrest. She was not here; she was gone. So were you. And so they found you."

Sextus.

He supposed he could blame anyone but Julia, anyone at all. He had to remember what she had done, though he still believed the part she played had been forced. He did not know if the magistrate would accept such a reason.

He had the power to pardon, but would he commit such an egregious act of circumventing the law?

"Your wife is a robber," said Lychicus. "But I think she will get out of this, Signor Emperor. She always manages away to slip out of the most perilous situations. She always finds a way to wriggle out of danger and emerge stronger."

"I wish I had your faith," Publius wanted to say, but instead he remained stone silent.

All he could think of now was Julia, his wife, locked in City Prison. He had a feeling he'd hear from her soon.

"Although you are aggrieved," said Lychicus, "there is a war going on. There are decisions to be made. Will you accompany me to the Cabinet of War?"

~

The Cabinet of War was a side room of the Council House, just below the top level. Arches and columns surrounded the circular chamber. There were portraits of great battles in history, the Thenoans against the southrons, the Khazidees against the Kheroans, even one of the hero Theron in his lion's skin.

A legate was there in military garb. So too was the Magister of War.

In some ways, these people are my enemies. But not now. Now they are my allies.

Lychicus, with the aid of his cane, sat down on one of the chairs.

"You help lock up my wife," said Publius. "Then you expect my aid."

It was the emperor's lot.

"Signor Mamercus," said Lychicus. He would not even acknowledge the comment. "Explain what has gone wrong."

The legate spoke. He seemed to be a hardened man of war, and old, with much gray hair mixed among dark blond.

"The city of Lornatium has broken away," the legate said simply. "They were Friends of the Empire. Now they wish to be free of our influence."

Let them, Publius wanted to say. But he knew it was not that simple.

"I know what our emperor would want to do," said Lychicus, "but our laws have made clear no Friend of the Empire can break away. We must ensure compliance. We must declare war."

The city of Lornatium was on the sunny southwest coast, a place of mild weather and happy climes. It was part of a league of cities, colonies of the Eastern Kingdoms that had established themselves long before the Imperial invasion. They considered themselves part of the East, but were friends of the Empire… or, rather, Friends of the Empire.

"We can revoke the law," said Publius. "Allies should not be forced into the fold…"

Lychicus smiled darkly. "If you believe passing a law with thirty bickering fools is difficult, try repealing one. It would take a miracle. Or will you break the law again, Signor Emperor?"

"No," said Publius. "No, I will not. But our legions are in Eioli, all those that are available. We have no more troops. No more resources."

"We must raise more, then," answered the legate.

"And will every young man of the Empire be a man of war?" said Publius. "Will we send every last one of our young blood to battle?"

"We must follow the law," said Lychicus simply.

And even if Publius wanted to disobey, he knew he could not.

~

That night, a special session of the Imperial Council was convened. War was declared on Lornatium and the league. It seemed every town in the peninsula was now an enemy.

Legions were called for; the Seventh Anthanian, now, adding to the number, the Fifth Nichaean, the Tenth Kerundian.

It was so; and Publius could not stop it. War there would be, and conflict. War there would be, and bloodshed.

Chapter Thirty

Empress Julia

Julia's cell was dark and damp.

She had not been afforded special accommodations.

She was in her satin gown, the one she had bought. And she was cold, yes, she was cold.

I do not belong here, she thought. *My crimes were not my own.*

They had called her a murderer, though she had no idea where they'd gotten such a baseless assertion. She had never spilled blood, never in her life.

She felt faint and lightheaded. She hungered for bread, for cake, for anything but the dry fare and the slop that the prison guards served.

She wanted to be out, to have her day in court, to face the consequences for what she had done.

But instead she was trapped in the darkness.

Darkness she was trapped in, yes, darkness, and she could not get comfortable. She was alone in her cell, but amazingly she wished to be with others, even the type of person locked in City Prison.

And she could not help feeling that the punishment did not fit the crime, that she did not deserve this.

Through the dim light of the windows she could see the cot that had been provided her, a cot of rough horsehair. The guards would not tell her when her trial was; she wondered if was part of a plot to make her uncomfortable, to torture her.

She had seen, in her youth, councilors charged with bribery; more often than not they were allowed house arrest, with guards posted at their doors. But things seemed to have changed, and to some she was seen as an enemy, a traitor to her class.

She prayed then, to the gods in heaven, silently, under her breath. She knew she was not guiltless. But this was too much for her to bear, and she was nauseous amid the flagstone flooring, the chips and holes that had collected water, but above all the darkness, the deep darkness.

And so she called up her powers. She attempted to leave. She felt her projected form drift upwards.

And more than ever, she felt the presence of the monster in the north.

Across the sea she flew, in the middle of the night, and the breeze was churning up the waves.

In her form she began to sink downward, and she saw that she was caught up in a storm. Sailors were there in a distance, hurrying to and fro from the deck, trying to escape. But they could not, no, they could not.

And dawn was rising over the sea, a red and glorious dawn.

Chapter Thirty-One

Empress Julia

Guards were stirring her awake, prodding her with spears. "Julia," said they, "your food."

The slop was as unappetizing as before, but she was ravenous with hunger. And so she took the bowl in one hand and the spoon and in the other. She shoveled it down, gulping it quickly, and found that it was interspersed with pork cracklings and thickened with lard.

If she were in a better place, where she belonged, in the Imperial Palace, she may well have thrown up. But instead she devoured every bit, and when she was done, licked the bowl clean.

The guard offered her a helping of water.

She was still ravenous, still starving, and when she closed her eyes she dreamed of great torte cakes and candied oranges, icing-covered cakes with mounting levels up into the heavens. But she was not there now; she was at her nadir—the nadir of her life, or at least, so far.

She did not belong here, she thought in a fury, in this dark and dank room, so cold, so chilled to the bone. Why was she not treated like the councilors? Why had they turned against her?

How she missed her room, the silken curtains, the paintings, the busts, the white marble floor. She was the empress; she deserved better.

The guard was staring at her, and the way he was staring at her made her uncomfortable. His eyes were dark, his face ruddy. But there were guards behind him; nothing would happen to her. Everything that would be done would be seen.

"It's quite cold in here," she said once she had made a halfhearted attempt at sipping the water. "And the cot is terribly uncomfortable."

"You are in City Prison," said the guard. "What do you expect?"

"I am the empress," Julia insisted. "You ought not to talk to me like that."

She wondered if there had ever been precedent, if ever an empress had been hauled off to prison and treated like a common criminal. She had never been treated so in her life, never so poorly. It had been the worst night's sleep in her life, and she thought she deserved better.

"You are Signora Empress," the guard answered. "But I am doing my duty. My orders are from above."

"Don't speak of the gods so flippantly," said Julia.

"No," the guard said. "Not the gods. I do not rule the prison, Julia. I receive my orders from the White Throne."

Julia harrumphed and finished the water, then slapped it back into the guard's hand.

But his words lingered. The White Throne. It was a term for the office of the Imperial Palace, for the emperor especially. It was considered improper for the emperor to interfere in the urban cohorts' business. All were meant to be equal in the eyes of the law, August, common, Knight. But would Publius break that unspoken norm? Julia had a hope he would.

Chapter Thirty-Two

Emperor Publius Corvus

"Will you free her?" said Lychicus as they walked through the Anthans Corridor.

"She deserves better than how she's been treated," said Publius, "and I've never seen the urban cohorts throw a councilor into prison."

They walked by the bust of Anthans, then of Hordo and Ansolon.

"But no," Publius answered. "I will not intervene. At least, not yet."

"A good answer," said Lychicus.

It struck Publius that, by some accounts, he was cavorting with his mortal enemy. The office of emperor was a strange thing.

~

A special council had been convened; at high noon the bells struck furiously and by the time an hour had passed the councilors began to filter in.

Publius sat upon the White Seat.

And the man standing before the councilors Publius did not recognize. He had on his head a pointed hat of scarlet cloth, and his tunic was colored bright hues of green and gold. His breeches went down to his calf and were tight-fitting, colored yellow; his shoes came to curled points.

Had they brought a jester? Surely not.

But no, it was not a jester, and when he spoke he spoke boldly.

"I come from Lornatium," said the man, "to declare

officially that we are ceasing our Friendship with the Empire.

"We have given orders to expel your troops."

"Orders," Lychicus demurred.

The clerk was scribbling furiously; the Legis lingered in the shadows.

"And who will protect your town without the Empire's help?" said Lychicus.

"Our mother city, Tharta," said the emissary. "We have sent for her aid. We expect she will not exact a price for her friendship. There will be no cost to our allyship. We are of one blood."

"How simplistic you are," Lychicus sneered.

Tharta was the greatest city of the Eastern Kingdoms, home to great wealth and luxurious palaces. Publius had only heard of it, that gleaming city across the sea, where gold statues shone on roads of white pavestone.

"There is a cost to everything," Lychicus said, "and there is a cost to breaking our laws."

"You will meddle in our affairs no longer!" cried the emissary.

"Guards," hissed Lychicus, "arrest him."

The Council Guards ran in and seized the emissary by the arms. Their blue plumes and blue capes contrasted starkly with the marble of the August chamber.

And Publius was appalled, yes, he was appalled. It was a grave offense to do harm to an emissary, against the laws of war and reason. But perhaps, it was the desperation of the lost war In Eioli and other towns breaking free that led Lychicus to do this.

It was rash. Perhaps, in normal circumstances, objections would be raised.

"This is against the law!" the emissary shrieked. "This is against all custom!"

"It is against the law to revoke your Friendship with the

Empire," said Lychicus, "and so you are not an emissary but a co-conspirator, a functionary of a criminal enterprise.

"Take him to City Prison! Tell the soldiers posted in Lornatium that they are to disregard the orders."

And at that Publius could take no more. "It is my purview to command the armies, Signor Speaker. They do nothing without my command."

The emissary was shrieking as he struggled, but bit by bit the Council Guards were foisting binds upon him.

"And will you break the law?" said Lychicus.

"It is mine to command the armies," said Publius.

As the emissary was hauled away, screaming, Lychicus perked up with the help of his cane, and a dark smile was on his lips.

"Signor Legis," said he, "I propose a law, an order that the soldiers stay in Lornatium, that they remain in that town in perpetuity."

The law was passed, twenty to ten, and even Marcus Corvus voted for it.

How powerless Publius felt, how powerless he was to effect change.

War there would be, war, with his consent or without it. Lornatium had no idea what was coming, but Publius had a feeling the Empire did not, either.

Chapter Thirty-Three

Empress Julia

Night had fallen; all light had vanished from her cell windows.

She had eaten her slop and a hunk of bread, and her stomach was growling. At times she felt nauseous. When she didn't she was hungry, starving in fact, dreaming of the feasts of her youth: butter crumbles topped with cream, mincemeat pies and sponge cakes. That was what she dreamed of as she sat there, huddled over, shivering.

Amid the pitch blackness, there was a loud slamming of a door and scattered shouts. A faint luminescence heralded the appearance of a lamp, carried by a guard. There were four guards in fact, four guards with broad shoulders and billowing plumes on their helmets. Was it the Council Guard?

The man they were restraining was protesting loudly. She could only imagine who it was.

They walked by her and Julia thought of calling for them.

It was unjust to keep her here, in the darkness, without any idea of when she'd see daylight again. But she could not wait to present herself before the people. She could not wait for her trial, for her deeds to see sunlight but also to present her case.

Would Publius get her out of here? She had her doubts he would break so strongly with what had been done before.

The guards were now in the distance; the lamplight had faded.

But Julia was not done.

Quickly, more quickly than she'd ever done before, she called up her power, let its iciness infuse her, and felt herself drift away. Then in her projected form she darted down the dark corridors and caught up with them.

They were Council Guards all right, Council Guards with blue plumes on their helmets and blue capes on their backs.

The Council rarely imprisoned anyone, and when they did was usually in the Council jail. Who was this man, she wondered? Who was he?

As she got a closer look, she noted his strange clothing, the cloth shoes that came to points, the cap he wore on his head. She knew it then, the ceremonial dress of Lornatium and the slight accent he had, the protestations and the invocation of the god Alabastrus. And she wondered why a man of Lornatium was being housed here, and treated with such cruelty.

The Council Guards spat at him and then slammed the door of the cell shut. He was whimpering in a pile.

And at that moment, Julia chose to reveal herself to him.

For a moment, as was always the case, she was wreathed in brilliance, and as he beheld her he cried "My gods!" and fell prostrate.

"Get up," said Julia, "I am no goddess, nor am I their messenger, at least not in the way you think."

And his reverence and awe evaporated in that moment, replaced with wide eyes and trembling hands. "So you are a ghost?"

"No," said Julia, "not exactly."

He was shaking all over. His eyes were shallow.

Julia touched him with an incorporeal hand.

"I am no ghost," Julia said. "I am a mortal, but I am appearing to you. And I want to know why you're here."

"Why am I here?" His fear had not quieted; his voice was cracking as he spoke. "Guards! Guards!" And like that the Council Guards were back.

Julia relinquished her power and she fell backward into her body, in the blink of an eye. It was among the shortest journeys she had ever taken. But whoever it was, she sensed ill intent. And she sensed she had not seen the last of him.

Chapter Thirty-Four

Emperor Publius Corvus

The night was cool on the Great Porch, and Publius' mind was going crazy.

He had in his hand a goblet of red wine. He was trying to relax, but thinking of Julia and Julia alone.

He turned, and saw, to his surprise, someone there, a man in a dark black cloak, with dark twinkling eyes.

Sextus.

No, it was not Sextus. It was in fact his brother Marcus, and as he drew near Publius felt a little better, a little comforted by his presence.

"You are dressing strangely," said Publius, "or have you in fact become an agent of the Empire?"

"Are we not all agents of the Empire?" said Marcus, "you especially."

"You seem dour, Publius. Can you tell me what is wrong?"

"What is wrong?" Publius murmured. "What is wrong?"

The cloak of jet black wool was one his brother had recently purchased. Money had begun to trickle in to the family's coffers; he was clearly replacing his wardrobe.

Publius peered into his brother's eyes. "Julia is in prison," Publius said, "and I fear she is dead."

When he told his brother of Julia's supernatural powers, Marcus seemed inclined to disbelieve.

"Projection," Marcus said. "What is that?"

"It is difficult to describe," Publius answered. "I do not understand it.

"But if she were all right, I think she would be appearing to me. I think she would let me know how she was, that she was safe, that she was being well cared for."

"Perhaps," Marcus began, and strode forward.

The lights of the city were below them, and the glassy sea.

"Perhaps she is angry with you," Marcus said.

"Why would she be angry?" Publius asked.

"Because you are not doing all you can to rescue her," Marcus said.

The words stung Publius. He had been following the example of the emperors before him, following custom and law and regulation. He was not to intervene in the work of the urban cohorts. He was not to intervene, even if it involved his wife.

But on thinking about it, it was true. Perhaps, she was angry. Perhaps, she was many things.

Perhaps, she was in danger, more danger than she knew.

Sextus frightened him and he didn't know what to make of him. He had begun to wonder if Sextus had a hand in Marcus' election. He had begun to wonder if Sextus was dangerous, if he had ulterior motives. He had begun to suspect Sextus had tipped off the urban cohorts. Yes, Sextus was involved in everything, and nothing was done without his hand.

It was ridiculous.

"Angry," Publius murmured to his brother. "Angry. I worry about her. They will not tell me the day of her trial."

"Perhaps, even the magistrates do not know," Marcus answered. "They are disorganized."

"And that is an injustice in itself," Publius said.

He wondered if the Red Hand cultists, locked up in the same prison, would recognize her, if they knew she had forsaken the religion. He wondered if the prison guards were mistreating her. He wondered, he wondered. And still he would not commit to intervening. But his resolve was weakening, the longer he didn't hear from her.

Publius stepped forward. The breeze was blowing in great

gusts. The clouds masked park of the sky, but the moon was brilliantly visible, a crescent, a sliver of heavenly light.

He turned northwards and walked up to the very edge of the Great Porch. He could not see Eioli, but he could think about it. There had been no news for several days; the city's allies had tried to break up the Imperial siege but had been driven away. And then what? What had happened? What happened next?

Marcus put a hand on his shoulder; he had walked up to the edge as well.

"Marcus," said Publius, "why did you vote for that war?"

"For the war in Lornatium?" Marcus said. "There will be no war. They are weak. They are dependent on us. They've forgotten how to fight. They've grown limp."

He turned peered into his brother's eyes. The redness of them had begun to fade. He had stopped his spice habit, it appeared, or so Publius hoped.

The words of his brother had not reassured him. "Weak. Dependent. Can't fight," Publius repeated. "That is what we said about Eioli. That is what we said about the Ugars."

Chapter Thirty-Five

Aulus Meridius, Legionary

A loud boom lit up the night.

The fire had rekindled, the fire in the Imperials' hearts.

And real flames there were, real flames in the distance. Those seemed to have rekindled as well, and in the darkness of the night the burning buildings were like beacons.

They had breached the gate; they had knocked down some of the makeshift fortifications. But they were dealing with a human wall, now, a wall of masses of Ugars crammed together. Everyone in the city was a warrior; they would fight with their last breath, with everything they had in them, to protect their home.

A woman came screaming, hurtling over the barricades. Her eyes were wild with rage. In her hands were twin knives; a child was strapped to her back. *"Ya Belphior!"* she was saying in her native tongue. *"Ya sha jaaran!"*

The legionaries were hesitant; the man next to Aulus slammed her with her shield and she went hurtling to the ground.

In close quarters they fought. For three consecutive days and nights they had tried to breach the gate, to push past this human wall that was as motivated as it was desperate.

The legionary next to Aulus stabbed the woman Ugar, and Aulus winced. He knew there was no choice; they could not let her be.

And the Ugars swarmed, and grabbed her dying form.

And there were drums, yes, loud drums, a steady rhythm beginning. Horns and trumpets lit up the night. There was a sound like whirring wheels, wheels grinding against stone.

Aulus had been sure of victory. But they had tried and failed for so long to breach the gate, he was beginning to think victory was impossible.

The fire withers.

The drums were growing louder. There was a sound of roaring flame, and a burst of heat.

And by that heat a thing that perhaps had always been there became visible: a statue growing hot, turning molten, turning from a silhouette to a blazing warning of danger. It was a statue of the Ugars' god Belpheor.

And at the sight of it Aulus was sickened. At the sight of it he remembered what had been done, what he had allowed to happen. And at its brazen face, now glowing, he was sick with grief and fear.

There was a scream; the woman who had been injured, and her babe, had been thrown upon it.

There were shouts of indignation among the soldiers, disgust at the horror of it, at the cruelty.

Aulus braced himself for plagues, for tormenting winds, for chattering spirits and sores opening up on his skin.

But instead there was nothing except anger, outrage at the horror of what had been done. And the fire rose, and the legionaries slowly seemed to be making up ground.

The fire rises once again.

And the legionaries swung their swords, heaving their shields together. The poorly armed Ugars began to retreat.

There were far-off screams; a faint cry.

Dozens of dark shapes appeared on one of the city's hills.

And in the instant the tide turned.

"Bulls!" Aulus said. "Great Bulls of Phaegor!"

One of the metal bulls gored the legionary next to Aulus; another legionary breathed in its poisoned breath and fell limp. A great slaughter was had; horns of retreat were blown.

Bulls… Great Bulls of Phaegor.

The legionaries were scattered away. In field and fen they attempted to regroup. The siege had been broken, and what a massacre had occurred, what slaughter. The fortifications surrounding the city were the death trap they had built for themselves, and Aulus had barely managed to hurtle over the palisades.

Bulls… Great Bulls of Phaegor!

Chapter Thirty-Six

Aulus Meridius, Legionary

The horrors of the night lingered, the terrors of shouts and screams, of soldiers mowed down by Ugar cavalry.

But Aulus was in one piece when the sun finally dawned. He was wounded, haggard, tired to his very soul, but he was alive, and in one piece.

The light was shades of gold and red. He walked alone.

He was so thirsty he was worried he would collapse; he was so hungry he worried he would faint.

He was beaten. And now his old hatreds had returned, his hatred for Eioli and Ugarit. No one deserved destruction more than they.

He staggered through the gold hills. He prayed to the god of the underworld, to whom he had consecrated the Rite of Devotion, "Will you help us? Or have you lost all power?"

The earth seemed to tremble; Aulus fell to one knee. No, no, his head was swimming. He had just imagined it.

And in the distance, amid scattered brush, a smattering of pines were growing, a cluster, a miniature forest. It was a sign of water in a desolate land.

~

The pond was dirty, colored brown, surrounded by ferns. The sun was rising and reflecting its light in the dark water.

Aulus was thirsty enough to drink this filth. And as he stepped forward, he saw a worm wriggling in the muck, and wondered if he were hungry enough to eat it.

The water was dirty, but it was water, and as Aulus cupped

it in his hands and slurped it down he felt refreshed. He drank and drank until his stomach ached. He drank until all thought of thirst had left him.

And then he looked up, and across from him in the pond, was an Ugar with a bow.

Aulus grabbed his shield, heaved it over his body. He braced it against himself. He would not surrender himself to the Ugars or he would be liable to be sacrificed.

But the Ugar did not shoot. And from the ferns and the darkness of the pines more Ugars emerged, warriors in chainmail and bearing spears, dozens and dozens of them. Aulus had no choice.

He stood up, dropped his shield and removed his sword. He lifted both hands above his head.

"Shaga," said one of the Ugars. He was wearing a conical helmet with a skirt of mail that fell down his back. His clothing was dark black and deep purple. He was the leader.

Aulus did not resist as they jerked binds upon him. He looked up to the heavens. He wondered if he would live. He wondered if he would survive this. But he knew the chances were slim.

The Ugar party began to drive across the hills. They were riding on chariots pulled by teams of horses. The thundering of their wheels was like a storm.

The sun had arisen; daylight was here. And Aulus was bundled up in a flea bitten blanket. They had not allowed him to eat. They had not given him so much as a bit of waybread.

His stomach growled as he sat on the chariot, as he watched the hills and forests go by. And as they went by he thought of his wife Falernia. He thought of his daughter Claudia and his son Horatius. What would they think if they knew this was his end, taken captive, perhaps sacrificed to the Ugars' god. Horatius, now nine years old, would not know the horrors of what that meant, but perhaps Claudia would.

I will never see Claudia marry. I will never see Horatius don his tunic.

There had always been a risk of that, always a chance. When one joined the legions, it was a gamble. Some did not survive to retirement. Others found violent ends even after they left in peace.

"It was a gamble," he whispered, under his breath, to Horatius, though the boy was miles and miles away in Imperial City, likely with his tutor or with his friends. "It was a gamble that did not pay off."

~

In the warm afternoon sun, Aulus woke with a start. He had been napping. And he could see that he was on higher ground, on a great hill, and swarms of Ugars were gathered there, Ugars dressed in armor, with spears. Horses there were, oxen and asses. Prostitutes were there as well, women with painted faces that clearly knew an opportunity when they saw one.

Aulus, in his thirty-three years, had not once betrayed Falernia, not even when he was posted half a world away in Khandara. He had been faithful. And he was sure that Falernia could say the same.

There were fires burning among the camps.

And to his shock, there was an Imperial walking amongst them uninhibited. He was in his glossy steel armor, his helmet with the red crest.

And there were other Imperials—yes, there were others.

One of the Ugars came around the chariot. In a thick accent , he said, "Get out!"

And he cut Aulus' binds.

Once firmly on the ground, Aulus looked about. Amid the darkly-clothed Ugars, Imperial legionaries were here. These were members of the besieging party, allowed to roam free.

He pulled aside an Imperial.

The legionary was blue eyed and traces of blond hair escaped his helmet. He was wearing his breastplate.

Aulus was free.

"What is going on, brother?" he said.

The legionary was slow to speak, as if hesitating to respond. "We are here…" said. "We are free… Prince Barca…"

He was at a loss for words, apparently. He quickly disappeared into the crowd.

~

Prince Barca was on a makeshift throne. He was dark complexioned, with thick black hair, with a coronet on his head and a long flowing silken robe of red. When Aulus introduced himself as a centurion, to his surprise Prince Barca granted him audience.

"You were not captured," said Barca. "You were rescued."

His throne was makeshift, built of wood, easily rolled this way and that, or hooked to teams of oxen.

"You have turned against your people." That, to Aulus, seemed the only explanation.

His guards surrounded the throne, guards in heavy mail and conical iron helmets that only showed the eyes.

"In a way," said Barca, "but not in truth. For one of yours has been held captive in the city. And she is beautiful, and she needs my help.

"She has hair of gold, and eyes of blue, and she wears a fine white gown. She seems to glow when she appears to me. And she is lovely.

"She calls herself Ulpia. Do you know her?"

"No," Aulus answered truthfully. Ulpia was a strange name. And it seemed this Barca was deluded, but delusions could be used to the Empire's advantage. Delusions could be used to change the tide of the war.

"She is so lovely… and she says if I enter the city, and rescue her, then she shall be my wife.

"First, she said, I must gather the remnants of the Imperials. Then we strike!

"I know my father's kingdom. I know my father's city. I will make quick work of them. His army will soon be reduced in number. They are going to strike the heart of the Empire. They are going to strike Imperial City."

Imperial City had never been conquered; it had never been so much as besieged. And at the thought of it Aulus began to panic, at the thought of his wife Falernia, his daughter Claudia, his son Horatius. He knew what cruelty the Ugars used against their captives.

"I must go!" said Aulus. "I must warn them!"

"No," boomed Barca, and for the first time there was harshness in his tone. "No Imperials leave the camp. We take the city. We rescue Ulpia. And then she shall be my wife."

Chapter Thirty-Seven

Emperor Publius Corvus

How lovely was springtime.

Tomorrow marked its beginning, the festival of the Rite of Spring. And in better circumstances, if the Empire were not engaged in war, and the empress were not in prison, the emperor would make a day of it and celebrate it with the people. But as Publius peered out his bedroom window, he knew he could not. For though spring was lovely he could not feel it. Though the sun would shine and the warmth would return, though the hills would be green and the trees and the flowers would bloom, he was in a winter he could not escape. And he was grieved that this all happened to him, grieved that this life was what he had been dealt. And he wished he had never donned the mantle of the Empire. He wished he had never gone to training. He wished he had stayed home, with his father Caius Corvus, with his sisters and his brother.

But he had not. He was emperor. His wife was in prison. The nation was on the brink, and he had no way of steering things right.

And so he fell to his knees before the window, and clasped the symbol of Hieronus in his hands. And he asked the gods for help.

The sunlight was filtering in. Far below, he could see the hippodrome and a series of chariots racing by the course, but the stands seemed sparsely filled. It seemed the gravity of the moment was not lost on the people… wars in Ugarit and soon in Lornatium. An empress imprisoned. An emperor unprepared and unready.

"Help me," he said to the gods, to Hieronus especially. "Help me."

"Publius." He had left the door open. Lychicus was there,

an old man leaning on a cane. He seemed distressed. And by his wispy gray hair, by his wrinkles, by the weakness of his gait, it seemed he was too old for this. But he had always seemed so.

Publius stood up from his prayers and faced his sometimes-enemy and sometimes-friend. He knew the news would not be good.

"The legions have scattered again," Lychicus said.

Publius' heart sank.

"And an army of Ugars is on its way to our city."

Now was not the time for despair, nor the sinking of hearts. "We must act," Publius said, "and we must act quickly.

"We convene the Council of War."

Chapter Thirty-Eight

Empress Julia

Dark was her prison cell; dark were her dreams.

And Julia, sitting there on the rough stone, without a blanket to comfort her, wondered if she was wasting away, if her time was short. She knew she was losing her grip on things, her belief that things would get better, her belief that things would work out in the end. She knew the trial would not be easy. But she wanted to face the magistrate. She wanted to accept her punishment.

In the darkness of the cell, she remembered just what she had done, in the distant past but also recently. Out of a wrong belief about her own nation she had joined the Red Hand cult; and now, out of opposition to the nation's enemies, within and without, she was doing her best to aid it.

She had told Prince Barca her name was Ulpia, her mother's name. She had promised him things she would not give, and so, there was a bit of deception to her actions. But he—thinking she was in Eioli—had promised to gathered the scattered remnants of the legions. There, they would be waiting for Publius when he got there. They would be there for her husband, yes, they would be there, even if the law treated Julia harshly, even if she lost her freedom or her life.

The breaking of the army was not the Empire's fault; the legions were well armed and well equipped. From Latera to Peregoth, from Agornesis to Riva the best of the best joined their ranks.

No; the breaking of the army was because of the dark deal the Ugars made. It was because of the monster desperate to break free. The land of Ugarit was haunted; there was a dark spirit in every grain of every patch of soil. And goodness demanded war.

Rightness demanded war. If ever Julia escaped from this predicament she'd found herself in, she would make it her mission to see it through.

And so she shut her eyes. She did not know if it was the morning, or the afternoon, if it was the daytime or the evening. She only knew she was hungry and cold.

She sensed someone there, at the door of her cell. And before he spoke she saw him, the guard from before, the guard who had looked at her in a way she hadn't liked.

But over time she had seen his intentions were pure.

"Signora Empress," he said. "Your trial is tomorrow, on the Rite of Spring."

The Rite of Spring. Dark memories surrounded that day. It was the day she had fled, the day she had run away under false pretenses. It was the day she had well and true left her old life behind and become an agent of the Red Hand. It was the day she had taken a step into the abyss.

She tried to remember what had happened afterwards. She had met Publius, her love. She would not have known him. But she would also not be here, in prison. She would not have had to pay for her crimes.

"Signor Guard," Julia answered. "Thank you. I look forward to seeing justice, whatever that entails."

"I shall pray for you, Signora Empress," the guard answered with a smile. Then he vanished into the darkness.

The Rite of Spring. The escape. Red cloth. A red dawn. Her heart had become a tempest. A flood of memories returned.

Soon it will be all over. Soon, one way or another...

Chapter Thirty-Nine

Emperor Publius Corvus

With the aid of his legates, Emperor Publius Corvus had made his preparations.

In a way, the emissary from Lornatium had won. The legions that guarded Lornatium and the other towns of that league would withdraw. For the City was in peril. And the City was the Empire's crown jewel, the very heart of her people.

And with his decision, even Speaker Lychicus agreed. The departure of the legions would ensure they would secede, at least for now. It would ensure that in the interim, they would not be Friends of the Empire, that they would govern free of Imperial rule.

And that was what he had wanted, but now it annoyed him; now it angered him. A law had been passed, a law that could no longer be fulfilled.

In the Council House, Publius was standing before the thirty councilors. Rows and rows of old men with white hair stared down at him, rows and rows save his brother Marcus, who was the youngest of them all. Over their snow-white tunics sashes of purple were laid. In theory all powers of the government came from them; and their powers from the votes of the people.

"Men of the Council," Publius said, "I regret to inform you our worst fears are realized. The legions have broken once again, and it is my personal belief that we must use greater than mortal weapons to defeat Eioli."

There were some puzzled looks among the gathered councilors. The speech had sounded much better when he spoke it in the mirror.

"It is my duty to command the armies," Publius said, "to guide their movements, to raise them. As this body asked I have commanded the creation of three new legions.

"But an Ugar army is on the march. The City is unprotected. We are evacuating our legions from Lornatium and its league, and I must personally lead them.

"You have forbidden me to leave the city. I ask that I be allowed to lead the armies. I ask that you revoke your demands. The people must see their emperor in battle. The people must see this war be won."

Speaker Lychicus appeared reluctant.

But in the end he agreed, and with a majority of the Council consenting, the laws were revoked. He was allowed to leave Imperial City. His freedom had again been won.

~

In the stables of the Imperial Palace, the greatest of the horses had been set aside for him.

He was a mighty white destrier, a stallion with a flowing mane.

And with the aid of the palace servants, they put his barding upon him, armor upon armor, forged of dark steel. It was the warhorse Publius would ride to confront the Ugars. Publius' fate would be tied with that of the soldiers; he would not retreat.

And so, when the armor had been laid upon the destrier, and his white body was covered with iron scales, the servants helped Publius into his steel sabatons and his greaves, and fitted great gauntlets over his hands. Over his chest they laid a suit of mail, and on his head they laid a helmet with a sideways purple crest, the symbol of the emperor.

In his hands they placed *Imperium's Rebuke,* the ancient sword of the emperors, and on his back they tied his shield of red.

Then, to his face they pushed a polished mirror. "All well, Your Excellency?" said one, a woman.

He was a man in armor, a dark giant of iron. And he bore the sword of the emperors. What would he have thought, just months ago? What would he have thought, just days ago, if he had seen himself now?

It was now night.

~

The Imperial Guard flanked him, bearing torches, several dozen in number. Behind were a select group from the urban cohorts and several centuries from the First Lateran Legion.

They would meet with two legions and rendezvous at Raven's Point, a village north of the City. Then they would strike, and gods willing, take the Ugars by surprise.

Chapter Forty

Empress Julia

Julia was in the dark, in her cell, and the window up above was pitch black.

She heard the rattling of keys, which stirred her from her stupor.

And then, amid the blackness, a dark shape took form.

"Julia."

She recognized the voice at once, that wretched Sextus. She could now envision him, his dark hair, his dark robe, his inky-black eyes.

"We must go," said Sextus, "we must go at once. You will not escape your trial alive. Men have been put to death for lesser things than what you've done."

"I am no man," Julia answered, "I am a woman. A Seánus.

"But that is no matter. I will hide no more, Sextus. You aren't all-powerful... one day the Council will know all about you and your associates. They will know about the mountain shrine."

Sextus paused in silence. "Ever insolent, ever proud... Julia Seánus, you have more of your father in you than you know."

"Good," Julia said. "I loved my father. I still do."

Sextus was silent, stunned perhaps by the audacious words.

But Julia had foresworn the Red Cult. She was deeply sorrowful at what she had done. And now she had foresworn Sextus and his agents as well.

"Be gone!" Julia said. "Do not come back, Sextus. You cannot help me. You cannot control everything and everyone. You are less powerful than you think."

She felt his hands upon her, she felt him slam her against the stone of the wall. She sensed his lips just inches from her own.

"Never again, Sextus," she said. "I am empress, the wife of Publius."

"That oaf," Sextus uttered, and released her.

Yet Julia knew so much, about Sextus and his men, about the lonely shrine on the dark mountain. And she resolved, as Sextus disappeared from her in defeat, that if she were to ever see the light of freedom again, she would tell Publius all.

Chapter Forty-One

Emperor Publius Corvus

The village of Raven's Point was so small the term village seemed too big for it.

It was perched on hills, a collection of about a dozen homes.

And surrounding it were thousands and thousands of men.

Thousands were there already, and more were coming. At dawn the legions of Lornatium would arrive. Here, on this battlefield, the fight of the ages would occur, the moment of testing. Would the Empire survive? Would its people remain free?

Or would the City perish, and the monster that dwelt in Eioli rule?

~

The night was cool, and on the hills of green grass some two thousand men had set up camps. No fires were burning for fear of alerting the Ugars.

Publius, by now, had removed his armor. His tent had been set up, and he had insisted it be as spare and humble as the rest of the legionaries. After all, that was what he had been not long ago.

On the crown of a hill, Publius looked up at the moon, and saw the great expanse of the heavens, the stars, the faint clouds of light. Every night they circled about the earth in their procession, going from one end of the world to the other. Since ancient times when the gods fixed them in their places, since time forgotten, they had helped sailors navigate the sea and lost wanderers find their way home. They told farmers when to plant and when to sow. And they provided endless fascination to those lucky enough to sleep outside.

It was dark, and against the sound of the gentle wind the scattered mutterings of the legionaries formed a kind of steady noise. He was focused. He'd become committed.

When he ascended to the White Throne, he had promised the councilors Eioli's destruction. But now he thought that he needed Julia. More than mortal weapons would be needed to conquer Eioli. More than mortal weapons would be needed to extend the Empire's grip over Ugarit, and therefore the peninsula.

Dark was the night. Dark had been his dreams. Fear he no longer had, only commitment, only resolve and focus. If he perished he would perish with the legions. But he would not perish. He would overcome. He would conquer.

To his knees he fell. He lifted his hands. He started to pray.

And then there was the sound of loud galloping. He turned and saw it was a rider in official garb, one of the relay riders who carried quick messages from the capital.

What now? he thought. *What ill tidings will I receive?*

~

In the dark of the night, he broke the Imperial seal and allowed the letter to unravel. On the top of the parchment the symbol of the Imperial Council was stamped in black ink. He shuddered at the thought of it, those thirty fools who held the nation hostage, those thirty fools who seemed to agree on only the worst of things. He wished the Council did not exist; he wished the emperor were elected directly by the people. But it was not so, nor would it be.

When he read the letter, his curiosity turned to annoyance.

"A proclamation for the Rite of Spring," was all he bothered to look at.

The Rite of Spring was an ancient holiday, a holiday everyone in the Empire and probably elsewhere celebrated. Yet somehow it could not be official with the emperor's signature.

He took the letter to his tent and procured the quill from his desk. He laid the letter on the wood. He dipped the quill in its ink.

And it was only then that he saw the handwritten note scribbled in, in handwriting he instantly recognized as Lychicus'.

"*Publius,*" the note was scrawled, "*Julia is on trial tomorrow. Know that I am watching things.*"

Publius did not smile. Instead he signed his name, finishing unfinished business that the Council should have reminded him of. The Rite of Spring was proclaimed for the year 211. It seemed that no parties could be held, no family gatherings could be held, without his approval.

The courier took off at a gallop in the middle of the night. The relays would carry the letter back to its place, well before dawn.

Chapter Forty-Two

Empress Julia Corvus

The dawn was not red, as it had been in last night's dream, but as she was poked and prodded, forced along through Imperial City's streets, her eyes were straining to adjust to the light.

People were gathered on the street to watch as the guards shoved her roughly. People were watching her, gawking, some glaring, some staring. She was being treated like an animal on purpose. She was guilty even before the jury handed down its verdict, at least in the eyes of the people.

She did not glare back at them as she was jerked and forced forward across the street. The street's pavestones were rough, and it was difficult to find her footing. Guards surrounded her at all sides.

But what a crowd had gathered, how many faces, faces dark and light, Imperials and foreigners.

"It is the Rite of Spring!" she wanted to say. "Why aren't you at home with spring cakes and hippocras?"

But she did not. She was their empress and in a way she still loved them.

With more rough prods they forced her onwards. They were drawing near the place of her trial, an obscure location called Atlas Square that would nonetheless not provide anonymity.

An old woman with greasy gray hair spat at her. Her face was covered with boils. "Criminal!" she bellowed. "Criminal!"

But Julia only smiled in response, and did not react harshly. She was *her* empress too.

The guard prodded her especially hard and she staggered forward. Her foot caught against a stone and she fell cruelly to the floor. Laughter erupted amid the crowd.

I will be strong, she thought to herself. *I am their empress. I will be their empress until the jury condemns me to death.*

And she found herself weeping. Tears were streaming down her cheeks. She was so close to despair. In the darkness of the prison she had yearned for this moment. Now darkness and anonymity was all she wanted.

She took a deep breath; she gathered herself.

If only the prison guards would not cruelly prod her with the butts of their spears. If only her hands were not cinched in rope. If only the people did not assume she was guilty.

But I am guilty, she remembered. *I am guilty of all charges, save murder.*

On and on she walked, and she found she could not help but weep, she could not help but allow the tears to stream free. What humiliation, what scorn. Jeers surrounded her; angry faces looked out from the huddled masses, but some were laughing and mocking her.

She was prodded especially hard and stumbled, almost falling, but she caught herself. A man in the crowd pelted her with a stone.

How much longer? Atlas Square was a mile from City Prison.

People will gawk at me there. People will laugh. People will cheer for my death.

She had begun to tremble; her fingers were shaking. She was appalled at her situation; she was appalled at what she had done. She looked up to the sky and saw it veiled with clouds. The air was brisk. "Father," she mouthed, though he did not know if Marcus Seánus could hear her.

I am sorry… I am so sorry.

Her father was forgiving. Her father was strong. Her father was in a better place, a much better place than her own.

Grief was welling up in her, now, grief. She missed him.

What wouldn't she give to see him now? And to see Ulpia, mother, now long-dead.

Mother, mother…

She prayed to the gods as she wept, as she staggered down the road, as the roads became more and more roughshod, as potholes appeared and the guards drove her through poorer and poorer neighborhoods. Yet poor though they were, the crowds had not thinned, and the onlookers were from every class and nationality. They were stopping to gawk, laughing, cheering.

But she saw a man looking at her sadly and wanted to embrace him; perhaps he pitied her and did not hate her, perhaps he did not hate her like it seemed everyone did, everyone in the Empire and in the entire world.

She stumbled again, falling to the floor. Her knees were bruised, her dress tattered. She was injured and exhausted, aggrieved and undone. She could go no further. *Will they carry me if I refuse to move?*

No, they will not…

She walked on, staggering ahead. She walked on, wincing, weeping, knees throbbing, heart aching. Her grief was larger than her shame. She wanted her father. She wanted her mother. She wanted to be away from here, from these leering faces, these scornful words, these curses uttered from the side of the street. She had never been so embarrassed, and that was how the guards wanted it.

Embarrassment, shame, grief, and still she walked on, lips trembling, eyes streaming. Embarrassment, shame, grief, and she was like a lamb being led to the slaughter, eager for it to all end, however it would end.

The road led her past dilapidated apartment blocks, past overgrown gardens, past rows of palms and green hedges that blocked out view. She walked until her shoes were sore, until her legs ached. She walked to the place of shame, to her certain death.

In Atlas Square, the place of her trial had been set up. The benches that surrounded the court were packed with people. The magistrate had arrived. And like an animal, forced into a cage for a manufactured hunt, she was pushed forth into her box.

The guard tried her binds, to make sure she could not escape. It was an insult, she thought. They knew she'd never be able to leave. They only wanted to humiliate her before the crowd.

In her early life she had thought those charged with crimes were given a modicum of doubt. Now she could see it was not so.

And then she saw him: across the court, near the judge's dais, in the witness box, was Varro.

Memories flooded back to her of his evil treatment, his evil words, his beatings. Memories returned of his slurs, of his curses on the Seánus name, of his true belief that he was the Red Lord, and that Julia was a symbol of the Empire—a stain she could not excise.

Resolve replaced her grief. Resolve returned, and a faint kindling of anger. For he did not belong there, judging her. Whatever she had done, and there was much, it was nothing compared to what he had.

It seemed an hour passed; Julia stirred uncomfortably. It was hot.

At times she thought of the palace, of Publius her love. She wondered if he was sitting on a divan of fine linen and being fed spring cakes by palace servants. The Rite of Spring was a delightful time for most, but not for her, at least, not now.

She had no holy symbol to touch. She had only her own prayers when the magistrate strode forward. She prepared herself, but she could not prepare for the sound of his voice.

"Julia Seánus," the magistrate began, "the daughter of Marcus Seánus, an August of good standing, an emperor of noble character, and of Ulpia Seánus, née Ajax, a native of the Isle of Serpents, stands hereby charged with a count of robbery and a count of murder.

"Those on whose behalf I act, the State, refuse to accept any guilty pleas."

It was just as well; a plea would not help her. And she was not in the mood to confess, not when Varro was standing there, the one who had transformed into the most evil man she had ever known.

Well, there were worse men, she supposed. Her mind turned to Sextus.

"The case will be proven," said the magistrate. "I am sure the jury will see the gravity of your actions."

The jury box was opposite the judge from the witness box, and four men and four women were sitting there on chairs. Like all juries they were selected from the great masses of the public at random, so that the eyes of Lady Justice would be blind. The founders of the Empire wanted to be sure impartial justice would be done, even to an emperor or an empress. The emperor had certain protections against the law, but none such were given to his wife or family or coterie.

And she gently dabbed her eyes. She wouldn't let Varro see her upset. She wouldn't let any of them see her weep. She would be stoic, strong, defiant though she knew she had done wrong. Others had done worse, but she had done wrong.

~

"Julia Seánus." The magistrate was standing before a portrait. "She was born into the purple, fed by a silver spoon, reared in luxury and comfort. She spent her youth tagging along with her father when he was a legate, then grand legate, then Magister of Foreign Affairs. She was brought from place to place, always in the best of accommodations. Her travels allowed her to see the world. It instilled in her a better sense than others of what right and wrong was. She saw the barbarians of the north and their customs, how they would let infants to die in the snow. She saw the excesses of our cousins in the Eastern Kingdoms and their license. She saw the contrast between Imperial and foreign. And in the temple, she knew very well the difference between right and wrong."

Julia gulped. All that had been said was true. When would the lies start? When would they accuse her of murder?

"But in all this time, there was a secret side of Julia Seánus. For unbeknownst to all of us and to most in the palace and the Council, she was a budding sorceress, and as she grew older her powers grew stronger, and throughout the City people would claim to have seen her in dreams.

"And when she had become a young woman she had tired of this nation; she had come to see it as wicked. And when her friends told her about the Cult of the Red Hand, her initial curiosity turned into participation and her participation then into devotion.

"And so, on the day of the Rite of Spring, exactly one year ago, Julia and her newfound friends made their plot. In the night they smashed various objects and Julia carefully let her own blood, intending to stage a scene of abduction. With her friends in the Red Hand cult she finally departed the charmed life she had led. And her abduction would send the palace into a frenzy. Her reckless action would unintentionally lead to her father's death."

Unintentionally, he had said. It was generous but it was true. She had striven desperately to convince herself she did not know. She had tried so mightily to tell herself she had not put her father in danger. Maybe the magistrate was right.

Tears welled in her eyes. She had not done what was right. She had not been her best self. She had not been who she had aspired to be.

Oh, Father… to take your place. To be where you are, now.

"And though she may protest," the magistrate said, "though she is beautiful and may garner sympathy, she became a full-fledged member of the cult. Not only did she rob the moneychangers in Golden Square, she threatened them. She took charge of the cult's finances. She was as complicit, as responsible, as any member of the Red Hand could be.

"And as to the charge of murder, she killed, with her sorcery, not a body but a mind. She turned Tidus Sulpicius Varro, veteran and devout patriot, into the now-condemned monster he is."

Is that where the charge of murder stemmed from? She could hardly believe they intended to use that line of attack.

Projection was a matter of traveling in between spaces, of visualizing and establishing yourself in a place far away. She had no power to control minds. She had no power to change people, other than her own words.

But she realized, with the naiveté and inexperience of the jurors with supernatural matters, that it was a dishonest line of attack that could work.

~

The magistrate droned on and on of the evidence he had. Witnesses took the stand, bystanders in Golden Square and then finally the moneychanger himself.

He was a short man, standing in the questioning box. She recognized his auburn hair and blue eyes, and was filled again with regret.

"She was with others," the man said. "She was with others, but she was holding the knife. She threatened me. She forced the keys out of me. She threatened to kill me."

The magistrate was prying the truth out of him. She had indeed threatened him.

But at that point she had become a victim herself; by that time Maria Domina's men had beaten her, physically and mentally.

By that time she had become a shell of herself, a witless thrall that would do anything to avoid pain.

Perhaps, she thought, *I am not as guilty as I believed.*

By that time she had borne bruises all over her body; by that time she had been a broken young woman.

But there had been opportunities to escape, opportunities she had not taken. Though they had mistreated her, though they had beaten her, she had become as zealous as any member of the Red Hand. She was to be married to a Red Hand leader named Servius… thank the gods she hadn't.

"And how much did she steal?" the magistrate continued his questioning.

"Ten thousand *denara,* in gold and silver," the moneychanger said.

There were gasps in the crowd. Julia had been close to the Red Hand's treasurer; the theft had been one of the Red Hand's greatest windfalls, if not the greatest. It had funded more criminal acts and the purchase of weapons.

Weapons. Tears welled again.

The Day of the Knives. At that point she had had no part. At that point she had been changed; Publius claimed she had been turned into an otherworldly beast, a creature of the night with no control over her actions and only a faint memory of what came before. If anyone was a murderer of souls, it was Maria Domina and her master Tidus Varro.

"Ten thousand *denara* in gold and silver!" the magistrate repeated in an incredulous tone. "More than most will see in their lifetimes. And it was stolen and put to ill use."

The magistrate turned to the jurors in their box. "Nothing else needs to be said, unless you believe all these witnesses to be liars and a woman such as Julia to be pure and innocent."

No, Julia thought, *I am not pure or innocent. I have done things I regret. But I am not a murderer. Nor would I be a thief if Maria Domina had not broken me.*

She stirred uncomfortably in her seat. The air had grown hot. So many of the audience in the stands were examining her, judging her.

"What is wrong with you?" she wanted to shout. "It is the Rite of Spring. Hippocras and spring cakes await you, sugar gooses and goslings, honey wafers and chestnut pies!"

But she said nothing, nor did she stand up. It was the day of her trial, and whatever came next, she could not help. Death perhaps awaited her, the forfeiture of all her wealth.

Tears welled again, this time tears for herself. She realized, in all, that she did not want to die.

The moneychanger left the questioning box, and Julia's heart trembled as she saw Tidus Varro get up from his place. Would she really have to endure the insults of that blackguard, that cur?

And yet indignant as she was, she was afraid, and butterflies were flipping this way and that in her stomach—that was what it felt like. And she wanted to be away from here. Death was better than seeing him again.

No, seeing him again *was* death.

Tidus Varro walked across the court and sat in his place. He looked at Julia with a dark grin on his face.

He had been condemned to die; now he was trying to do as much damage as he could, to take down as many people with him as possible. He was cruel in life and he was cruel in death.

"Tidus Varro," said the magistrate, turning to the jurors, "was a man of great mettle, a legionary of the Knightly class who quickly climbed the ranks. Soon, after many battles, he was entrusted with the care of the emperor, but even then he was not satisfied. He eventually achieved the title of the Marshal of the Guard, the leader of every Imperial Guard in the palace.

"With a sober mind and a devoted heart, he took good care of the previous emperor, and eventually was charged with investigating the disappearance of Julia.

"And he pursued her with abandon… he made it his life's goal to find her. And find her he did, though he did not know she was luring him into the spider's web."

Stop, she wanted to say. *How dare you.* But instead she gritted her teeth. She remained quiet. She allowed the lies to pour out.

"You look at her." Varro was speaking now, that cur, that blackguard. "She is beautiful. But she is fierce and she is deadly.

"Before she put her spell on me, there was no greater patriot in the Empire. I served the nation with all I had in me, and then she laid on me her curse."

Julia strove so desperately to remain quiet, to give the modicum of respect that, in truth, was not due. She tried to remind herself that she would have her say, her moment to speak. She would have her time to defend herself.

"She called me to Saturnus Rock. She laid on my head a wreath. And she called me the 'Red Lord.'"

"Liar!" Julia screeched, and guards went to restrain her. The judge pounded his gavel.

"Silence!" the judge hissed. "There shall be order here…"

And Tidus Varro was smirking, that cur, that monster. He knew his words were false, didn't he?

"And because of that curse, because she ruined me, I plotted and planned the Day of the Knives… yes, I admit it now, but it was all because of Julia."

There were cross faces in the crowd now, some brimming with anger. Like a serpent he was, crafty, cunning, planning his words, manipulating the masses like he had before in his capacity as the Red Lord. Ever cunning, ever crafty he was, and Julia was filled with such loathing she ground her teeth together.

I will have my time… I will have my moment. And then, in all likelihood, I will have my death.

"This court is adjourned until one hour after noon," the judge said. "Signora Julia will have her defense as all accused do. The magistrate has rested."

Julia examined the faces of the jurors. She read in them confusion, but also uncertainty.

Chapter Forty-Three

Empress Julia Corvus

The sun had grown in strength.

It was now the afternoon. And like a lamb led to its slaughter, Julia was led back to her private box.

Some of the crowd had dispersed, no doubt due to the Rite of Spring. There were parties throughout the city, including a great gathering in Imperial Square; there were plays being performed on stages throughout the city. Not even the trial of the empress could fill every seat.

And it was a lovely day, yes, it was a lovely day, and the sun was shining. The sky was blue and spring was truly here.

What a day to learn you will die.

The judge pounded with his gavel. "The trial of Julia Seánus commences," he said.

~

It was Julia's turn in the witness box. Her defender, which every citizen in the Empire was entitled to, faced her in the light of the sun, and the sun's rays made him look like a messenger of the gods.

"Julia Seánus," said the defender, "let me ask before the people gathered here, before the jurors who will decide your fate, are you innocent or are you guilty?"

"Of theft," Julia said, "I am guilty."

The defender could not disguise his disbelief; this had not been discussed. She had pled initially innocent but now she had changed her mind. She would face the consequences of her actions, and whatever the gods demanded of her she would give, even her life.

"And what's more, though I am no murderer, I was reckless in my actions. I knew what the Red Hand wanted, to kill the emperor. I had hoped they would not slay my father. But when my father died, I was not surprised," Julia said.

There were gasps in the crowd, and audible hisses. A juror pucked her face. Disgust was all around, disgust writ on everyone's features, on the defender especially.

"What are you doing?" the defender's face read. "Do you know you are giving up your life?"

So be it. She would face the penalty. She had done wrong.

The defender was standing there, a while, in stunned silence, unable to believe the turn of events, disgusted at the actions of his client. Julia would not lie; she would not add deception to her offenses.

"But now that I have told you all," Julia said, "I will tell you another truth, none less true. Varro chose his own path! I, under threat of violence, summoned him to Saturnus Rock. I, under threat of violence, watched as the wreath of the Red Lord was put on his head.

"But his choices were his own. I did not alter his mind. I did not murder his mind or his soul. He chose his own path. I had nothing to do with his transformation; it came from within."

There were audible curses from Tidus Varro in the witness box.

"And as for me," Julia said, "I throw myself at the mercy of the court. I beg for clemency, as someone who knows what wrong she has done. But mercy I do not deserve, and I understand that.

"When I was young and impressionable, my friends led me astray. I thought at one time that I hated the Empire, the nation of my birth. But now I do not. Now I serve it. Now I oppose those who despise it; I work against those who work against it.

"I am Julia Seánus, once the emperor's daughter, now the emperor's wife. My life is in your hands. I do not deserve mercy, but I ask for it."

The defender's stunned face did not change a whit. She had told all. Every dark shadow, every dark secret, had been exposed to the light. She had joined in with a cult whose express goal was killing the emperor; now her fate was in the hands of the gods, and of the jury.

But if she had moved hearts, if she had garnered any kind of sympathy, the angry looks in the crowd and the puzzled glances of the jurors showed no sign of it.

I have done myself in. She had confessed. And she now realized she was not ready to die, no, not yet.

Chapter Forty-Four

Emperor Publius Corvus

All day he had made preparations, riding about from hill to hill. They were laying a trap that the Ugar army, he hoped, would walk into.

For an army to pass from the Ugar coast to the land of Anthania on the eastern shore, one normally passed through a great valley called the Riverine.

And on hills and in forests Publius Corvus had hid his troops, legionaries and centurions alike, equestrians and auxiliaries of archers from the Eastern Kingdoms. He had plotted this, and scouting reports that continuously reached his ears said all was well, the Ugars were following their regularly scheduled path.

Other news was not so good. The army they were using was thrice the size of the two legions with Publius. They were badly outnumbered, and every rebellious city had contributed some thousands of soldiers to Eioli's cause.

It was Publius' greatest test, the greatest challenge he had endured. And he would fight to the end; he would be the last to retreat. His fate was tied with this army, and with the Empire.

The sun was going down, and wind was on the hills. He recalled it was the Rite of Spring, and he remembered the good days of yesteryear, when the Empire was not in crisis, when the people would join together in parties and great gatherings. *Spring cakes, hippocras, sugar goslings…*

Horns blew, deafening horns, not Imperial horns but loud and blaring horns, the horns of the enemy.

And the horns were coming from all sides, from behind them and from ahead.

The Ugars had foreseen their trap. Who had told them?

Who?

Chapter Forty-Five

Empress Julia Corvus

It was dusk when Julia returned to her box. The crowds had largely regathered, but they were few. Tidus Varro was no longer in the witness box.

The jury had been talking for hours, but the judge had returned to his seat.

It will all be over, one way or the other.

She wondered if the gods would forgive her. She wondered if her father, now gone from her, was at peace.

The things she had done, though they were done under pressure, were unacceptable and deserved punishment. She could only imagine what the jurors thought; she could only imagine what they said. She resented that they were in charge of her life. She resented that they were the judges of her life, she, Julia Seánus.

One of the jurors, a male, stood up and handed the judge a tablet.

"Julia Seánus," he said, "the accused. Please rise."

Julia's stomach was twisting to knots. She could scarcely breathe. She could scarcely think.

But she exhaled when she remembered that, after this moment, it would all be over, for better or for worse. She would receive the payment that was due.

"On the charge of murder," the judge said, "the jury finds you not guilty."

Julia could feel not just months or weeks but years of tension leave her. Light came back to her, light in her soul, a candle relit, burning brightly, purging all her dark corners.

"On the charge of theft," the judge said, "the jury finds you guilty."

So it is true. There is justice in this world...

Chapter Forty-Six

Emperor Publius Corvus

The horns. *The horns!*

But Publius was wrong, they had not come from behind. All was well. The trap was set. And in the hazy horizon, the dark forms of warriors were appearing, marching countless in their number. They were like a sea of armored figures, as vast as the sea in Imperial Harbor, emerging warrior by warrior, battalion by battalion.

And beasts they had brought, bulls of immense size and at the head of the army a chariot pulled by horses.

So vast was the army, so impossible was it to fathom. How could the Ugar Coast—rich though it was—feed so many mouths and stomachs?

The army was approaching, heading toward the valley, towards Imperial City which lay un-walled and vulnerable. In that city, Publius' home, hundreds of thousands lived. By now the warnings had been sent to evacuate, to prepare to leave.

Thunderously the army made its way through the valley. They had, as yet, noticed nothing. In the army's wake trees fell and the earth seemed to quake under their stamping feet.

How could such a force exist, Publius wondered? How could so many people be in one place? And they all marched under one banner, the banner of the Ugars, of the divided cities that had put aside their squabbles and their wars.

Publius' nerves were on fire.

He had been deprived of his first battle as a legionary. This was his first experience in war. Would it be his last?

It was Publius' task to make the signal. But as he drew the trumpet from his back, he hesitated.

He watched and waited as the countless throngs made its way through the low valley. Impossibly distant were a ridge of hills, on the other side, where another legion was waiting. Would they hear Publius' horn?

Publius pressed the trumpet to his lips. He took the deepest breath he'd ever taken.

Then he blew until his temples throbbed, until his eyes bulged and his veins seemed to pop. The noise was deafening, a piercing, solitary, even note. He cast the trumpet aside.

In unison, the two legions descended.

There were cries of alarm in the darkened valley, loud screams of panic. The leaders of the Ugar battalions barked various orders, demanding that shield and sword be at the ready.

Publius, leading the equestrians, was followed by a cavalcade of men on horses, all armed with light shields and sword. "Forward!" Publius cried. "Forward, for the Empire..."

When the equestrians struck, panic struck the ranks of the Ugars. Those on the front lines turned and trampled those behind. The warriors began to disperse and flee, even as the legions made their approach from either side.

But there was no escape for them, no escape at all. The legions had sealed off the valley. This place would be their graveyard.

Chapter Forty-Seven

Empress Julia Corvus

It was almost night, almost dark.

Julia sat in the privacy of her box, knowing it was over. All that was left was to hear her punishment: death perhaps, or the sale of herself into bondage.

The crowds in the stands were now gone. Julia had been waiting for the better part of an hour.

And then there was motion in the distance, as the crickets chirped and the night noises formed a dark music. From the shadows behind the judge's dais, a man emerged, leaning on a cane.

And in a panicked moment, she recognized him as Lychicus, the Speaker of the Council with whom she had so fiercely quarreled. She was his foe. And now, he would speak on behalf of the State; on behalf of the State, the aggrieved party who owned the moneychangers' stand.

"The State of the Empire," Lychicus said, "has been robbed of some ten thousand *denara*. Such a crime must have a price. Ordinarily, such a crime would demand the sum plus ten percent, and if the victim could not pay, sale into slavery.

"But Signor Judge, Julia is not like the others. She can pay in a different way.

"All emperors and empresses are paid a sum, even after they retire. I demand the forfeiture of this sum in perpetuity. She shall collect no money, nor shall her husband, after Emperor Publius abdicates."

The judge paused.

There were so few in the stands, Julia could count them on one hand.

She realized it was a fair sentence, and far better than she feared.

She also realized what she had done to her husband, what she had done to them both. After he retired the emperorship, they'd have to find some other way to make ends meet.

"Signor Lychicus," she said in a fury of passion, "please…"

But she knew in her heart this was the best possible outcome. She knew in her heart this was what she deserved. But it was not what Publius deserved.

The judge spoke after his long pause.

"That is not what the law demands," said the judge, "but as the aggrieved party you have a right to make your petition.

"And the petition is granted. Julia Corvus, empress, and her husband, will receive no payment after her husband abdicates."

~

It was late at night by the time she returned to the palace. She had been returned to the prison, various documents had been filed and sealed with Imperial seals. Then she had been set free.

And the palace was dark, and it was lonely. As she walked through the halls toward her bedroom, it seemed more and more bizarre to see the isolated corridors. Where was the Imperial Guard?

She was halfway to her room when she caught sight of a palace servant, one she recognized, Kynthia.

"What is wrong?" she said.

"The palace and the Council have been evacuated," Kynthia answered in a hushed tone. "The place of their meeting is undisclosed. There is a battle being fought, and your husband is at the head of it. The Ugars are trying to make their way to Imperial City."

Her husband, fighting in battle. It seemed so unduly risky, to himself and to the nation. But it was something Publius would do. In his high-minded ideals of honor and duty, he would never put any soldier into harm's way where he wouldn't go himself.

Ah…

To gain her freedom and lose her heart would be worth nothing. She made her way to her bedroom, passing Kynthia. She prayed as she walked.

The room was dark; the lamps were cold and unlit. It seemed Publius had not been here in days. But on a table, in the moonlight that shone through the wafting curtain, she could see a meal had been prepared for her, a meal for the Rite of Spring.

A note was by the plate. "Julia," the note wrote, "you have no idea how much I've done for you. –Lychicus."

The spring cakes were stale; the hippocras was cold and showed signs of spoiling.

Julia ate in the darkness, thankful for her freedom and for her life, but hoping against hope she would not lose what she loved most in the world.

Chapter Forty-Eight

Emperor Publius Corvus

Back and forth was the rhythm and battle, hope and despair, momentum and retreat.

On horseback Publius fought furiously at the head of his men. Three Ugars had been killed by his hand, and his sword, *Imperium's Rebuke,* was wet with blood. His helm and armor bore countless scratches. Many times he had thought he would die.

But in the dark night, under a yellow moon, the forces of the Empire and the forces of the barbarian coast were clashing.

Shouts rang out, cries for the help of their god Belpheor.

But their "god" was not here, their "god" was elsewhere, underneath the spires of Eioli's temple where he slept.

And Publius fought more furiously than ever. The equestrians had driven into the heart of the Ugar army, and the legionaries had begun to press them from all sides.

Desperation was in the Ugars' eyes, but they were far removed from their dark magics. Their pleas for Belpheor's hope were in vain, unheard. Here the gods in heaven reigned; here their foul sacrifices would have no effect.

The Ugars were trapped; there was no way out.

The legion was beginning to squeeze them, to cut them down man by man, warrior by warrior.

And Publius looked up at the moon, and saw it was now ochre, more red than yellow. The stars were blazing brightly, and the constellation of the Eagle was above-head.

With a furious cry he drove forward, trampling Ugars underfoot, striking and slashing, piercing and heaving his enemies aside. And seconds turned to minutes, minutes to hours.

The battle was won, and the grass in the Riverine Valley

would grow well.

~

    In the daylight he surveyed the bodies. Crows were circling overhead, a whole host of them, hungry for flesh.

    And as to their victory, Publius could not help but feel a twinge of anxiety. He was not well.

    He recalled the redness of the moon and thought of the dawn. He thought of the monster yearning to break free and knew it was not defeated.

    The bodies had begun to rot under the sun's warmth. There was no means for the burial of so many bodies, nor was it customary for a victor to bury the vanquished. Instead these countless thousands would give life to the grass.

    Their armor would be removed and re-forged. The new legions being raised would be well equipped.

    Publius rode along the perimeter of the valley. He knew he would not return to the City. He would not because it was not wise. A resounding victory had been won; they would now march forth and conquer Eioli once and for all.

Chapter Forty-Nine

Empress Julia Corvus

In the light of the day, Julia fended off her anxiety only a little while, her worries that Publius was not safe, that his life was in danger. She did not want to bother him, but before noon—sitting in her bedroom—she realized she could no longer help it, she could no longer help herself.

And so she lifted up her hands and called up her powers. She let the magic infuse her. And she drifted into her projected form, into a form that was not substantial but that could be seen, and that could see.

Over the hills she flew, searching for any sign of them. She soared, hurtling on, to the Ugar coast, but there was no trace of them.

But there were tracks, grasses and vegetation that had been trampled underfoot, discarded bones and bits of trash that had been thrown aside. And chewing on a bone was a bull.

"Bulls," said she, "Great Bulls of Phaegor!"

Along the tracks she flew, soaring quickly, and the tracks to follow were easy, and impossibly vast.

In the Riverine Valley the tracks ended, and there, high above, on a hill, she could see her love alive and well, riding on a horse. He was dressed head to toe in steel, like a warrior of old. His horse was covered in steel scales with an opening for its eyes and nothing more. Compared to the other legionaries he was like a man of iron; but he had removed his visor, and she could see his face.

She drifted over to him, as if carried by the wind. With a shout she allowed him to see her, and he gasped.

"Julia," he said. "We are going to Eioli… there is no time."

"Remember what I said?" Julia wanted to shake him. "The

monster… he will not let the war easily be won. You must have me come with you, and with me one-thousand priests."

"Priests?" Publius muttered. "What good will that do?"

"We are not dealing with mortal weapons," Julia said, "but unnatural ones.

"Publius, I am the empress… I am your wife."

"Are you free?"

"Yes," Julia said. She could not yet bear to tell him what had been done to her, what had been done to him. "Yes, and do you remember our wedding? Do you remember our feast? Will you have me miss Eioli's siege? Will you walk into danger without me by your side?"

"It is inadvisable," Publius said. "But if you will have it done, I will return. And we will go together."

~

For two days and two nights Julia waited. For two days and two nights she prayed.

She asked the Council for her demands, and though they resisted they eventually allowed her to go, to repeal the law that forbade her from leaving, and to take with her one-thousand priests.

Chapter Fifty

Aulus Meridius, Legionary

The days had not been easy, the nights far worse. He hadn't slept hardly a bit since he reached Prince Barca's camp. All he could think on was Falernia, Claudia and Horatius. All he could think on was the Ugar army marching home, to Imperial City, to a city and a nation that had been ravaged and weakened by war, and that was ripe for the plucking.

He had drawn to the edges of Prince Barca's camp. The tents and the noise were far behind him. He could hear Ugar music playing, haunting melodies of the harp and cymbal. He was at a loss.

As he surveyed the hills, the mixed forests, the stone pines far away, he recalled the Rite he had performed, the Rite of Devotion that had appalled his fellow legionaries. He recalled the hatred that he had for Eioli, and knew now that it had been transformed to fear and panic. What would the peninsula and the world look like if the Ugars dominated it? What would the peninsula look like if the worship of Belpheor spread?

He looked at his hands, and remembered the horror at Devil's Dolmen. He looked at his hands and remembered what he had done, or at the minimum, what he had not resisted with all his heart.

He recalled it was spring. In the distance, clouds were drifting across the firmament. He wondered if he prayed the gods would hear him. He wondered, if he prayed, whether Claudia and Falernia and Horatius would be spared.

But he was alone, and the noise of the camp was behind him. He was alone, and his punishment was on him, his sacrilege, his dark and filthy deed.

"Signor Aulus?" A voice woke him up from his stupor.

What did Aulus look like, hunched over on the grass? What did he look like? He hadn't thought of it. He supposed it didn't matter. Nothing mattered, not anymore.

He got up and decided to make the best of it, to put on a brave face, to try to recover what little of his dignity he could muster. Having risen he could see the annoyance now, no, not an annoyance, a young legionary who had been his subordinate, one Quintus Marcus Rufus.

He was bright-eyed, Rufus. He had been over-eager to fight and some in the Red Century had found him annoying.

But he had been reassigned at the best possible time for him; he had been reassigned to the Holyoak Century, yes, that was right, the Holyoak. And he had not witnessed the horror at Devil's Dolmen.

He had not seen the eyes of Nivus, the eyes that bled. He had not stood aback in horror.

"Signor Aulus?" Rufus said awkwardly, and Aulus was stirred again out of his thoughts.

"Yes," he muttered, "yes, yes… it is I."

"Isn't it great news?" Rufus continued.

"What news?"

"You haven't heard? The legions have decimated the Ugar army in the Riverine Valley. The survivors scattered in a panic."

Yet Rufus' words seemed to trouble him nonetheless. Falernia, Horatius, Claudia—they were safe.

But was Aulus safe? Would news spread? Was anyone else in on the plot? Would they turn him in?

"Great news," Aulus said, and put on the best smile he could. "Great news indeed…"

He felt he was a traitor to the Imperial people. Under the instruction of his superior he had allowed foreign rites to happen. He had allowed the barbaric customs of the Ugars to be done.

No, no… I will not be discovered. Nor would he turn himself in. But within he had become a tempest. Within, a storm seemed to have taken root.

And when he shut his eyes he saw Nivus' bleeding eyes, and when he looked at Rufus' fresh young face he imagined sores opening on his skin.

Rufus was looking at him questioningly.

"Leave me be!" Aulus shouted roughly, and ran away, like a madman, yes, like a madman. He ran across the hill to the standing pool where he got his water. He looked into his reflection in the glimmering waters.

He could not see them but he knew they were growing. He touched his temples. He could not feel them.

Where were the horns growing? Where were the horns?

Chapter Fifty-One

Empress Julia Corvus

Standing before the bedroom mirror, with a servant girl at her feet, Julia carefully examined the platelets and the bun that her hair had been tied up into. She seemed to have lost fat in her body and so oils had been pressed carefully against her skin; it masked the wasting away she'd endured within the prison walls. Over her eyelashes she had dabbed Ink-of-Tyrrhenos, over her lips, balm imported at a premium from Khandara. She looked like she'd had on her best days.

She was garbed in nothing more than a smock. The next stage of her morning would be even more difficult.

"Hallë," Julia told the servant girl, "I am pleased. You have done well."

And Hallë rose without so much as a smile.

They were walking to the wardrobe when a familiar face greeted them. Publius, her husband, was standing there in the main hall, looking slightly exacerbated.

"Julia," he said, "the nation is in crisis, and…"

"And I must look well for the soldiers. I must look well for my fight."

Fight. What did it take to drive away a monster such as Belpheor?

Publius now looked incredulous.

"I will hurry!" Julia said.

She had purchased several gowns and dresses from the Harbor District since she'd returned from prison. She went through them at length, the brocades, the silks, the gold-and-silver tissues.

But in the end, she remembered what she was, an Imperial woman, the first woman of the Empire. And so in this most patriotic of quests, she saw her traditional white gown tucked away in the corner, a gift that had been passed down to her from her mother.

She took it from the rack and examined it.

It was a humble thing, plain, of linen that had been dyed so well and so repeatedly that it was bright as snow.

"What do you think of it?" Julia said.

"I rather like it," Hallë answered and there was no deception in her tone.

And so Julia laid it over her body with the help of Hallë, tucking in her arms, and cinched it with a rope belt of gold. And over her head she laid her white veil, the traditional garb of an Imperial matron.

To Publius' annoyance, she skipped over to the mirror. She was the striking image of her mother. Her clothing was radiantly white. She truly looked like an Imperial matron now, a most dignified and noble domina.

This is who I am, she told herself. *This is who I am meant to be.*

~

With Publius' hand in hers, she was guided matron-like, down the halls, as servants declared their departure.

"Our honeymoon at last," Julia whispered in Publius' ear teasingly, and a grin grew on his lips. "And not a moment too late!"

Trumpets pealed as they departed the palace, as the news was announced that emperor and empress alike were departing to oversee the war in Eioli, and would be satisfied with nothing less than victory.

Trumpets pealed as they stepped into their fine oak carriage pulled by teams of horses.

And trumpets pealed as the Imperial Guard followed them through streets, past proud highways filled with people, and finally through Imperial Square, where one-thousand priests were waiting.

Interlude II

The emperor was not fearful when he departed; no, he was eager.

And as he left down the great road, flanked by his guard, he had never been more sure of victory, never more sure of Eioli's defeat.

And so he sent a letter before him, along the relay of fast horses, that his offer to Eioli was revoked. There was no more chance for surrender, no more chance for terms. Annihilation and annihilation alone was what was offered; annihilation and annihilation alone was what they would receive.

Chapter Fifty-Two

Emperor Publius Corvus

The carriage was finely furnished, with a plush bed lined with purple silk. In the darkness lamps were provided, and in between bouts of lovemaking and glasses of fine wine, Publius and his wife began to discuss more than just the war.

"At our wedding," said Publius one night with a glass of wine in hand. He leaned over, sloshing it and almost spilling it. "I did not see any Seánus there. No uncle, no aunt. Only your friends from your youth, your friends from the City."

The coming war was now far from his mind.

"Seánus." Julia too had a glass of wine in her hand, but hers was almost all drunk, and the bottle was gone. "What a name. A founding family of the Empire.

"But as for my father and me, his brothers kept their distance. My grandfather practically disowned us."

"And why?" Publius said, and touched the hem of her gown.

"Because my mother, they said, was a barbarian, a tribeswoman from the Isle of Serpents…" Julia looked down sadly. "The House of Ajax was not a great house, and she was not a highly placed member of it.

"But her family had some means. They sent her to Imperial City to study. It was a chance meeting… she, a student of philosophy, he, a nobleman who was swiftly rising through the ranks.

"And she was good. And she was refined. But she was from the Isle of Serpents and my grandfather couldn't seem to forgive her for it."

Julia Seánus, not noble enough? It seemed preposterous to

Publius. She exuded nobility and refinement and aristocracy from her very being. Everything about her was like a princess.

And at the thought, Publius' mind turned to dark thoughts. If Julia were not noble enough, what did the Augusts and members of the Imperial Council think of *him*? He was technically an August now, but of no antiquity. The Corvus family was not there at the founding of the Empire.

He was a scion of the now-noble Line of Corvus, but did that make a difference in others' eyes?

What, indeed, did other Augusts think of him?

But it was no matter, he told himself, no, it was no matter at all. He was not just a scion but the emperor, the leader of the Empire.

There was a gust of wind; Julia looked up. At first there was a look of concern on her face, but it quickly quieted.

In the morning, under a cloudy pink sky, Publius looked out the window and saw they had gone off road, through rough terrain.

"What is this?" he yelled to the carriage driver. "Where are we going?"

"Julia's orders," the carriage driver barked.

Julia lay still asleep on their bed. He shook her furiously and she woke with a start.

"Where have you sent us? Where are we going?" Publius said.

And in the haziness of sleep and with winking eyes a smile grew on her face. "I confess a little trickery, Publius… Prince Barca I convinced to repatriate the old legions. There are survivors, a scattered remnant. We are headed to his camp."

By the time day came, Publius was out of the carriage,

riding on his horse. Before him were low hills stretching into the interminable distance, forests of pine and scattered ponds. He had grown hungry, but he was grateful not to be in his armor, that metal suit that made it so difficult to breathe and do ordinary tasks.

The carriage door opened and Julia flung herself out. She had torn off her veil and was now in her white gown. She had left scarcely at all in this long journey.

The legions had not followed the carriage along this detour, no, they hadn't. And Publius, as the trip dragged on, began to question her, and to question everything.

"There!" Julia pointed ahead. "Look! Up ahead!"

Beyond a ridge of hills Publius could see smoke rising. It was a camp if he had ever seen one. So much smoke was wafting up it had to be that of an army, a great force. It would help much in Eioli's conquest.

Beyond a low fence, thousands upon thousands of Imperial soldiers idled, some wearing their helmets and some not. Mixed in were Ugar warriors of varying dress, some with skirted helmets and chainmail and others bearing nothing more than spears and wooden shields.

Beyond the fence the carriage rattled. Its wheels were now caked with dirt and pebbles.

The Imperial Guard could not provide protection against such a force, if it were ever to turn against him.

But horns sounded, great horns, and trumpets and drums. There was the sound of galloping hooves, and in the light of the day Publius could see a cavalcade riding toward them. Mounted on a horse, bathed in white sunlight, was an Ugar handsome in form, with a crown of gold on his head.

"Milady!" he cried.

What is this?

Julia looked embarrassed.

What had she done?

"Milady!" Prince Barca said. "You are here... here at last!"

And at the way Barca was looking at her, Publius felt a twinge of jealousy and a flash of anger, burning hot. "What is this?" he cried, incredulous.

"Barca," said Julia, "you have done well. But I have made a promise I cannot fulfill... this is my husband, the emperor. He thanks you, and I thank you."

"Not you, then," said Barca, "but the child you are carrying, your firstborn daughter."

"The child I am carrying?" Julia repeated his words in an incredulous tone.

"I can sense it," Barca said. "I have five wives, I will have you know. If you I cannot have, your daughter I will."

"Enough of this!" Publius growled. "Where... where is the legate? Who is the commander of these forces?"

Chapter Fifty-Three

Empress Julia Corvus

She was still strumming her stomach, still touching her belly, still wondering, when the commander of the Imperials showed himself.

Handsome was he, sullen, dark of skin, with a scar across his cheek that surely women would love. But as he drew near in his gleaming armor, Julia was overcome with horror. Growing from his temples were two bull's horns.

"What is this?" she said, and was filled with revulsion.

"I am Hastatus," the legate said. "Manius Hastatus, the grand legate. I've been waiting for you, Emperor Publius, my signore."

And he knelt down, and yes, Julia was not just imagining things. She was really seeing this, truly, she was. From his head two great bull's horns were growing. And she was appalled.

"Signor Grand Legate." Publius managed to keep a cool tone. "Surely you know the question I am about to ask."

"Day and night I've prayed to my god," said Hastatus. "And these horns began to grow. I consider it a sign, a sign of our coming victory, my dominus, my emperor, my lord."

Publius remained silent. Julia touched his hand and fell faint; a dizzy spell had come over her, borne of anxiety and perplexion.

"Victory," Publius said at long last, after a long pause. "Victory… See to it that your men are ready before the noon hour. We leave and meet with the others. And then we march."

"Your wish is my command, my dominus," said Hastatus.

It was before midday when the legions assembled in their centuries. They had gotten all of their things, and on the edge of the camp, in the shade of the tree, Julia found Barca.

"I am sorry," Julia said, "that I promised something I never could give. But I was desperate."

A faint smile came to Barca's lips. "It is all right, my sweet. I am from Eioli but I am not of it.

"And that daughter in your belly... I sense greatness in her."

Julia blushed, and touched her stomach once more. "Thank you, Signor Prince," Julia said, "from the bottom of my heart, thank you. I will do my best to repay."

~

It was dusk when the four legions met on the road to Eioli. It was dusk when Hastatus was appointed grand legate of all of them. It was dusk, and the number of the soldiers was fourteen thousand.

They were not far from Eioli. Julia peered outside the carriage window, and saw a firmament with pink clouds. Publius' servants were helping him into his greaves; he had already donned most of his armor. It struck her then that her husband was again heading into danger, again heading into war.

At least I will be near him this time.

She laid a hold of the door handle. She opened it and hopped out, difficult though it was in her white gown. She walked over to her husband and kissed him. Then she announced in her loudest voice, "Soldiers of the Empire... the finest among the fine, before you go into battle there is something we must do. For it is not completely against men that you fight."

On the outskirts of camp, the one-thousand priests of various gods made their sacrifices. The blood of ten white heifers was spilled upon a wooden altar. Prayers were made, chants were sung.

And the legions departed, with Julia in the carriage, as dusk turned to twilight and as twilight turned to night.

~

It was dark and Julia was now covered in a cold sweat. She was alone in her carriage, now, and the soldiers of the Empire outside were so numerous that their marching was like an earthquake. At odd intervals trumpets would sound, followed by bellowing horns. Loud war-drums kept an eerie rhythm. Julia was guarded on either side by the Imperial Guard but she knew she was not safe; she knew whatever fate these four legions met, it would also be hers.

It seemed like hours before the carriage ground to a halt. Julia's breathing had become shallow and difficult. The legionaries were running now, and the sound of their running feet was like the beating of a thousand truncheons.

And she stepped out of the carriage, dizzy and faint. And she raised her hands, and she saw the dark outline of the city's walls. She was here in this accursed place, in this haunted earth. She had come to Ugarit as prepared as she could. And so she drew within herself as the legions stormed toward the gate; she called up magic and lifted up herself in her projected form.

Rising she was, floating upwards like a feather carried by the wind. She could feel fear coming from Eioli, fear and anger and despair. And she soared toward the city walls, and she now could see Eioli's temple, Eioli's temple where the monster lived. It was a hideous thing of spires and rough towers, an abomination of inhuman architecture. But she braced herself, and she drew within herself, and she soared toward the city to do battle.

An invisible barrier met her, a barrier of hatred, a barrier of fear. She could not push past it; she could not fly beyond the city wall. She was at a standstill—no, she was being pushed back. She was being driven away, back, back, back, toward her body, toward her physical self. She cried out and pushed on, and a little resistance gave way. But soon she was being driven backward again, though it was agony, and at last snapped back into her body, into her physical self.

Publius was there in the darkness ahead of her, astride his horse.

And Julia, Julia, her heart was racing within her chest. And she wanted to be anywhere but here.

"Publius," Julia said, "It resists me... I... I cannot—"

She could not finish her words, and then she realized truthfully how exhausted she was, how pained she was by her experience.

But if Publius was vexed he showed no sign of it.

And he was holding something in his left hand.

"Your necklace," Publius said. "I forgot to give it to you."

Her necklace! What a name to call her most important tool of sorcery, the family heirloom into which she had placed her essence. She rushed over to Publius, saying "Thank you," and took what she had called the Star of Seladora. She laid it around her neck, and as she did she could feel her focus sharpen and her power become more controlled.

As Publius galloped off toward the site of the siege, she drew up her power once more with greater focus and energy than she'd had in many months. She went soaring out of her body in her projected forms, above the army fighting valiantly at the gate. She went soaring, and what resistance there was she crushed.

She was soaring above the Ugar city, above its flat-roofed homes and shops. She was soaring, and when she came to the temple she burst through its windows, traveling downward, downward, downward into the spiral staircase.

The basement, deep beneath the earth, was pitch black. A residual feeling was left here, despair, anger, fear.

But the monster of Eioli had departed. Whether it had been driven away or it had left she did not know.

But in the darkness, Julia was alone. In the darkness, there was only darkness and nothing more.

~

Julia snapped back into her body. She adjusted her necklace, the so-called Star of Seladora.

And as she witnessed the soldiers, so young, so full of life, she could not help but gasp. They were numbered in the thousands, and they had taken a battering ram to Eioli's gate… Eioli's gate, which looked cobbled-together or hastily re-assembled.

Young they were, hale, handsome, in breastplates of iron and shining helms crowned with red. So many thousands, from the peninsula and beyond, had converged on this one spot, on this one rebellious city, this city that had enticed its sisters to lawlessness.

And Julia in her gown and her veil touched her breast, and began to walk toward the place of battle. The noise was deafening. Cheers and roars of exultation were heard rising above the night noises. Catapults were flinging stones with reckless abandon.

And with a great crash the gate of Eioli gave way, shuddering on its hinges and then collapsing into debris.

Julia could scarcely breathe, now.

But she could not help herself. She kept walking, though she was ill prepared, in her white gown. She kept walking toward the site of battle.

There were shouts of rage and loud trumpets. Buildings exploded under the weight of the hundreds of catapults; the sound of their sundering was like thunder.

And Julia was faint, fearful of what was coming on the world. Julia was faint, fearful of what she was witnessing.

"Signora Empress!" a member of the Imperial Guard shouted from the distance. "Come back! You are not safe so close to the battle."

"I must witness this!" was Julia's answer. "I must see this all for myself."

There were shouts triumphant; the armies began to pour into the city in a stampede. Trumpets sounded, and so did war drums—great booming timpanis.

And Julia was caught in a spell of faintness again, a spell of dizziness, of anxiety, fear.

But she tried to steel herself, to focus, as she saw the thousands upon thousands of soldiers sprinting into the city. The resistance was gone. Eioli had resisted for years with its neck stiff and proud; how quickly that resistance had given way, how suddenly it had vanished into the night.

And Julia drew closer, yes, she drew closer, as the legions sprinted into the city, and soon she was where they had been, on the edge of the city walls.

Hulking forms were there, immense horned beasts. The light of the fires glinted on their scales. They were the great Bulls of Phaegor, now mortally wounded, their bodies stuck with spears like pincushions. They were dying slowly, and their hateful black eyes had lost their life. The Imperial legionaries had done this.

And Julia was walking ahead, as if led by a spirit, as the anguished cries of the Ugars lit up the night. She walked on amid the sounds of battle, as the last resistance had given way. Eioli had fallen, and how suddenly it fell.

Soon she was past the crumbled gate, walking trance-like

through the streets, in nothing but her gown and veil.

In one town square a statue was blazing, still molten but losing its heat, and in the statue's hands was a burnt figure. Yet their "god" Belpheor had not answered. He had not saved them. The Ugars had been left to die.

And on Julia walked, past legionaries fighting warriors, Imperials fighting barbarians. The fires all around her had turned night to day. The entire city was burning, and the streets were red with blood.

She looked up and saw a cloud drift away. The veil of the moon was lifted, and the moon was red, bright crimson. Julia staggered back, faint again, faint with fear.

A thunderous boom echoed all across the city as a catapult struck the temple. Against the red light of the moon, an entire tower cascaded downward in a shower of bricks.

The Empire had won, and what power had been turned against Eioli. Julia was breathless, and tried not to envision such power turned against an unworthy foe.

Eioli had fallen, and how sudden was its fall.

The moon was as blood, a sign in the heavens though Julia did not know of what.

Her breath had become shallow; breathing at all was a strain.

Shouts of triumph were rising up, shouts of triumph everywhere.

~

It was morning, in the tender light of the sun. Julia was lying on a blanket. "I dreamed," she told the hazy form hovering above her, "that Eioli was conquered… that the moon was red."

"It was no dream," said the Imperial Guard. "We found you fainted in the city… in what was the city…"

A lump grew in Julia's throat as she sat up.

Smoke was still rising up from Eioli. It was now day. And crews of Imperials were heaving bits of the wall away, chucking them down below.

"What is this?" Julia said.

Other Imperial Guards were with him, other Imperial Guards surrounding her. Hordes of Ugars were outside in the daylight, hordes of Ugars tied with binds. Would they be sold in the dark slave markets of the south? Julia prayed not.

"Publius' orders," the Imperial Guard went on. "No stone will be left standing. No memory of Eioli will remain. It will be erased from history."

It didn't sound like Publius… it didn't sound like Publius at all.

She looked over at the Ugars, so many of them, women and children. She wondered how complicit they were in the worship of Belpheor, in the dark rites, in the rebellion and the lawlessness. She said a prayer for them silently. She hoped they would not be harmed.

She rose up and steadied herself, and took a deep breath.

The Empire had won… it had won. So why did Julia not feel like they had won?

"Tikal and Hoda are next." Tufts of brown hair escaped the Imperial Guard's helmet. "They will all be erased from history."

That does not sound like Publius at all…

Victory! Victory… She wondered where her husband was. After the war was over, she hoped they'd both forget the matter.

The walls were being reduced, and the faces of the soldiers were jubilant, when she found Publius riding on his horse. He by now had removed his helmet and his armor, and he wore only his tunic and his breeches. His sword was clipped to his side.

"Julia," he said softly. "It is good to see you."

But his eyes were distant; he was looking through her and

past her, not at her. The war and the Empire were all that were on his mind. He was a good emperor, a much better emperor than she'd thought he'd be, and she had thought well of him before.

He was focused… or was he disturbed?

~

By the time the noon hour fell, Julia realized something was wrong. Someone told her a legionary had made a promise to Yblis, the god of the underworld, in the manner of the Cymbri tribes.

In the Imperial tent, Julia pulled Publius aside. He was stone-faced; it seemed he had already decided.

"You don't have to do this," she said. She touched the collar of his tunic. "You don't have to…"

"Oaths to the gods are not to be taken lightly," Publius said, "not even the Cymbri's god, the god of the underworld. What he promised, the god of the underworld must receive."

There was no talking him out of it. There was no convincing him. The Rite of Devotion was to be performed, though it was foreign, though it was consecrated to the lord of the depths.

Julia, accepting defeat, left the tent into the fresh air. The sky was blue, and Eioli was smoldering.

Eioli had fallen, and how sudden was its fall.

Chapter Fifty-Four

Aulus Meridius, Legionary

"Claudia." Aulus was stuttering like a madman. "Falernia! Horatius!"

They had bound his hand in binds; they had dragged him near Eioli's ruined gate. The emperor Publius had declared himself judge, jury, and executioner.

"Claudia," Aulus said again, mad with panic. "Falernia. Horatius! Please."

He was surrounded by legionaries, and could not escape. Near the edge of the wall, workmen were digging a great pit.

He had made a promise he did not want to fulfill, a promise made before Eioli's fall when it seemed unconquerable.

"Claudia!" Aulus screamed. "Falernia! Horatius! Please!"

His answer was a length of cloth stuffed around his mouth that was quickly yanked tighter. And as the heat of the day grew, as he stood there, he felt his body on its own relax. He remembered his friend, Varius Tycho, sacrificed to the Ugars. He remembered the city's insolence. He realized the Empire had triumphed.

And for a moment he regained his stature; for a moment he regained his poise.

Then they grabbed him and hurled him into the great pit and he hit the ground, and blind panic rose up once again him.

Through the cloth in his mouth he tried to scream. He jerked wildly in his binds as the first shovel of dirt hit his legs.

Eioli had fallen... how sudden was its fall!

Part Three

Chapter Fifty-Five

Empress Julia Corvus

Julia stood before the great drawing room mirror and touched her belly.

She had returned to Imperial City only recently and now she had confirmed that she was with child.

She adjusted her blue gown of fustian, and dabbed at her hair, tied up in a caul. She had had dreams, lately, happy dreams, of sunny shores and gentle winds, of a life long and well lived. It was only the beginning of her husband's administration, and many years were yet to come.

With an indefatigable ally in Councilor Marcus Corvus, she was sure Publius' emperorship would be safe. And already they were making plans to go to Paradise Gardens this summer.

Just yesterday Publius had returned from the war in Ugarit; every last city had been captured, and were being demolished one-by-one.

It was an extreme measure, but one Publius could not be swayed from.

And outside, signs of summer were growing.

~

Through the corridors of the Imperial Palace she walked, and a gaggle of servant girls followed her.

She found her husband, as she expected, on the Great Porch, and the sun was shining on the marble columns. Far away sea gulls circled the harbor, and below in the streets the city bustled with activity. The wars in Ugarit were slowly receding from memory.

He did not look at her when she approached, but when she drew near he spoke to her: "They want to give me a triumph, you know."

"A triumph!" Julia said. "Who?"

"The Council."

Triumphs for victorious generals were a common sight in the Eastern Kingdoms. When Anaxander conquered Khazidea, he rode through the city on a chariot pulled by white horses.

"So let them do it," Julia said. "Perhaps, our people need to see a celebration after so much strife."

The people had, indeed, been through much. Throughout the war there had been much terrible news, even the evacuation of the government from the City. Legions had been called, legions upon legions, and the "barbarians" of the Ugar Coast had dealt them countless devastating defeats.

"It seems," Publius said, "so un-Imperial."

"Will you turn Speaker Lychicus into a foe once more?" Julia asked.

Publius turned, and there was a gentle smile on his face. The sunlight was beautiful on his black hair, and the marble columns of the porch were blinding white in the light of day.

But the doors to the Great Porch were swept open, and a man came sprinting outside, collapsing to his knees. He dripped with sweat. "Emperor, my dominus… Latera is burning! Latera is burning!"

Chapter Fifty-Six

Vello Lychicus, Speaker of the Council

In the hallowed Council chamber, Speaker Lychicus cross-examined the messenger.

"It is burning!" was all he had managed to say. It seemed he were stricken by a dark spell, or some vile fever.

He was trembling all over, like he had witnessed a horror. He was an Imperial messenger—that had been confirmed—but he was acting the part of a madman, someone you'd see begging on the street.

"Steel yourself! Steel yourself!" Lychicus said.

The messenger's whole chest was heaving.

"The Thartan Kingdom... the Thartan Kingdom..."

~

By the time the news was wrung out of him, it all began to make sense.

The town of Lornatium, in the far southeast of the peninsula, had broken free of the Empire and begged the help of its mother city in the East.

What surprised Lychicus was that the Thartan Kingdom had answered, and a force stronger and larger than any the Empire had ever faced was marching south to fight them.

On its way south the vast army had set fire to the border town of Latera.

And at the news Lychicus' heart was beating at a more elevated pace than usual.

"How many?" Lychicus asked the messengers. "How many soldiers are with the Thartans?"

"It seems," the messenger said wide-eyed, full of terror, "that the whole world has come. That the whole world has come to fight the Empire. There are more than I'd ever thought possible."

At Lychicus' coercion, new legions had been raised for the purposes of besieging Eioli. But in the end they would have a different use. They were stocked with young men from all across the peninsula, and veterans too: the newly named Fifth Nichaean, Tenth Kerundian, and Seventh Anthanian.

On a field of battle they would face their greatest test. The Eastern Kingdoms were ever hoping to expand their power, to add new territories. But the Empire, across the sea, they had left alone because of distance.

The Eastern Kingdoms treated them, at best, like an unruly younger cousin. They did not take the Empire seriously. They would soon.

"Men of the Council." The messenger left through the Council Hall's great doors. Lychicus with his cane walked out of his seat, down the steps, to assume leadership of this meeting.

In the center of the Council House he stood, and he raised his hand. "I move that we assume emergency powers. I move that the Council take charge of this war."

The emperor had been through enough. In the end he had gotten lucky. Such a war only the Council was capable of undertaking.

The vote was unanimous, thirty to none. And now Lychicus, as commander-in-chief, would make his preparations. Lychicus, as leader of the armies, would see this war through.

Chapter Fifty-Seven

Empress Julia Corvus

On the Great Porch they had shut the door, and so the open space they had to themselves. Publius had pulled up chairs on the porch's edge.

The air was warm. They were both reclined. Julia placed her leg on Publius'.

"What shall we call her?" Julia said.

"Her?" Publius said. "How do you know it is a daughter? Do you really believe that oaf Barca?"

Publius still seemed angered by her ploy. But it was a ploy that had led to Eioli's capture.

"If it is a girl," Julia corrected her question, "what shall we call her?"

In olden times, an Imperial father had the power of life or death over his children and his wife. If a babe did not satisfy him, he was within his rights to dispose of it. That was still true, in the matter of law, but most did not practice it. Most fathers were respectful of their family.

There was a long silence. Perhaps, Publius did not want to answer, did not want to dignify her question with a response.

But eventually, he spoke.

"Julia," he said, "not long ago I was a legionary. I was one of the common. I was training in Blue Eagle Camp.

"And I was deceived, and you appeared to me…"

"Must we talk of it?" Julia said in a hushed tone.

"I want to know why you found me. I want to know why you saved me."

The incident at the mountain shrine was a test, a test she had helped him pass. But what he wanted to know she could not tell him. She did not know why she took a liking to him. She did not know why she followed after him, why he appealed to her. Was it not always so for love?

In her sojourn for the Red Lord, in her search, she had seen the agents' test being undertaken. She had seen Publius. She had found him. What more was there to say?

But why indeed? Why of those thirteen young forms, running in the late summer sun, did she like Publius best? Of all those thirteen soldiers of the Empire, why did she choose him?

Such was love, she supposed, or what would become love.

"I don't know why I liked you best," Julia said. "But I did."

Was the matter settled? Silence then reigned, and for a while they merely peered beyond the marble columns to the sea and the city below. Such was life, their life. This was the path that had been decided for them.

Dangers remained, as they did for all emperors. Crises could erupt. The world could be turned on its head. But for now they were safe and they were sound, for now they were alive.

~

In the afternoon, news reached them. The last surviving members of the Red Hand cult had gathered at a village called Eximenius. There they would make their last stand.

Chapter Fifty-Eight

Vello Lychicus, Speaker of the Council, Commander-in-Chief

Days Later…

The legions were marching in their hundreds, the Seventh Anthanian, brave and strong. Of guerilla war the Eastern Kingdoms knew nothing, no, they would not be met like barbarians. On the open field the two armies would meet.

And drums, Vello Lychicus heard, loud drums, timpanis sounded by the legion.

Pit pat, dum dom the drums sounded and the legions stepped to the beat. *Pit pat, dum dom* they rang, and the sound of their marching feet was like a constant roll of thunder.

On his chariot Lychicus, the commander of the armies, rode. He rode with a sober bearing in the heat of the day. He had placed the command of the legions in the hands of his legates. And he would ride on, to the field of battle, the rising versus the dominant, the new against the old, the Empire versus the Eastern Kingdoms.

Pit pat, dum dom the drums sounded. *Pit pat, dum dom.*

~

It was a day of blistering heat when the armies of the Eastern Kingdoms appeared. Behind them on a high hill was a burning village. And their number was hard to comprehend.

From one side of the horizon to the other the army stretched, and their brazen helmets were topped with blue crests. They were one machine, row upon row of soldiers with their hoplons tucked to the left and their spears to the right. They formed a wall, a human wall, but on their flanks, interspersed among them, were beasts that defied description. They were immense things with thick gray hides, and bulbous horns emerging from their heads. Rhinoceroses they were called and the Thartans had laid armor over them that sparkled gold in the sunlight. On the beasts' backs were riders of immense size.

They were meant to shock, they were meant to cause fear. From the depths of the south they had pulled those beasts, from some forgotten jungle that no cartographer has ever mapped.

But if the Seventh Anthanian had any fear of the mighty rhinoceros, Lychichus could see no sign of it.

The legionaries had by now stopped their march.

And out of the ranks of the Thartan soldiers a rider came galloping, a rider garbed in purple, with a headdress of diamonds on his head.

"Surrender to us our colonies in Lornatium, which you stole," said the rider, "and His Majesty the King of Kings Pardes will not harm you."

At the words Lychicus huffed. This messenger bore the attire and arrogant bearing of the southrons.

"Turn back!" he shouted. "Or there will be no quarter!"

"No," Lychicus said simply.

And at the word, as if he had summoned some dark spirit, the Thartan soldiers began to run. The rhinoceroses began to charge.

And the Imperials of the Seventh Anthanian Legion held firm, locking shields together, trusting each other as brothers. Arrows flew. Blood was shed. And the fighting carried on from the daytime until well into the night.

~

Victory it was, and what a victory. In the morning light

Lychicus could see it, the Thartans dead or scattered.

The Empire had paid a cost as well.

But in the morning sun, in the gentle light, the breadth of their victory became clear. Crows were circling overhead. Thartan bodies lay like a sea and the rest had scattered. From field to field they would be hunted down.

What a humiliation the Thartans had earned for their king.

Would such a victory ever be won again by the Empire? Against an infinitely vaster foe, against a foe more ancient and rich and well supplied, the citizen-soldiers of the Empire had prevailed.

Victory, and what a victory!

Victory, and what a victory it was!

Chapter Fifty-Nine

Emperor Publius Corvus

Publius' horse was treading the rough earth, its hooves grinding up dirt as it galloped. The last cultists had fled from Eximenius to Pulcher, from Pulcher to the Chrysum Forest, and from the Chrysum Forest now to the coast, to the western sea. Publius had made it his mission to hunt them down. The Red Hand cult would be no more, nor would it be remembered. Like the Ugars it would be purged from the history books, all texts burned, all tablets smashed.

The woods were opening up. Below on the coast he could see them, on the sand of the shore, and with the Imperial Guard he circled about and plunged downward into a deep ravine.

The leader of the Red Hand, the one who called himself Gray Hood, was with his dozen remaining followers, the last who truly believed. He was wizened and his face was marred with scars. One eye was white and soupy and sightless. He was the picture of ill health.

And behind him Publius' men thundered, the Imperial Guard and a portion of the urban cohorts.

Every member of the Red Hand had in their hands bowls, and the bowls were filled with a black liquid.

"This is your last chance, Gray Hood!" Publius said. "Your last chance to surrender…"

"The Red Dawn is at hand!" Gray Hood screamed. "The Red Dawn is at hand! And when it comes, we shall awaken, and the Red Lord shall see that you die, Publius, yes, he will!"

And he thrust the bowl to his lips and drank deeply of the black liquid. His followers did the same.

Publius watched as one by one the members of the Red

Hand cult fell down and were convulsed with seizures on the sand.

Publius wanted to weep, at such wasted lives, at those whom Gray Hood had led astray. Like a hungry lion he had found vulnerable victims, and taken them to their ends.

"Let us go," Publius said.

But the earth seemed to tremble. The twilit sky was brilliant as the sun sank beneath the water. The skies, full of clouds, were red and purple and gold, as brilliant a sky as Publius had ever seen.

"Is it the Red Dawn?" said an Imperial Guard.

"No," Publius said. "The Red Dawn is not at hand and it never will be."

~

One morning, days later, the skies were blue and sunny, and gentle winds were blowing through the palace windows. In the morning there was food, and there was music. In the morning there was Julia his love.

Chapter Sixty

Empress Julia Corvus

On the steps of the Temple of All Gods in Imperial Square, Julia stood waiting. She was the empress now and she was on the steps alone. Crowds filled Imperial Square, from one edge to another.

It was the first military triumph in generations, and her husband Publius had to be convinced to accept the honors.

And as she waited for his appearance, she smiled for the people and waved.

Carts and carts of gold, pulled by oxen, were making their way down the thoroughfare. Carts and carts of gold, taken from Eioli, were being ferried through Imperial City's streets, and trinkets and coins were being tossed into the crowd.

Julia was not without regrets. She wondered in the end if justice had been done, to herself and elsewhere.

And still, on some mornings, she would awake and wonder if the Red Dawn was at hand.

But it was not so. Every person in the world had a purpose, even the evildoers for judgment. Every person was a cog in the grand machine.

And this was her purpose, she thought, at least it was her purpose for now. For now she served her country, for now she was the empress.

On and on they went, the carts filled with gold, and it seemed there was no end to their number. When they passed down the great avenue, they began to veer away and assemble in the open space before the Temple of All Gods.

And Julia in her gown was there, on the steps before the temple, waiting for the arrival of their husband.

The carts went by the crowds, one by one, so heavy with gold that oxen pulled them, piled so high that coins would occasionally escape and a person would leap out to grab them. On and on, and the carts seemed to have no end, piled high with treasure and innumerable as they went by.

Julia wondered what her future would be. She pondered it, she pondered her purpose. For now she knew what it was.

The carts glimmered in the sun; rays of sunlight peeked through clouds. The crowds were cheering louder than before and then Julia saw why.

Members of the Imperial Council were walking down the way, as was customary in a triumph. Their wisdom had been needed in troubled times. At the back of them a barge was being pulled by oxen, a ceremonial ship, an ancient tradition of triumphs that was lost to history. On the barge what was called the Counsel of War sat, the Speaker Lychicus with his face painted blue and the trident of the sea-god Lorenus in hand.

Loud cheers echoed. And still Julia was lost in pondering.

She had told Publius of her punishment, of the blow the court of law had dealt them both. He had not been angered or annoyed; he had accepted it, and already they were making plans, already they were plotting how to survive.

The councilors were climbing up the great steps of the temple. Fifteen steps there were, and two councilors there would be on either side. The origins of the triumph were arcane and lost to history, but they were exact and prescriptive.

Julia thought of the moon above Eioli, the moon that glowed a bright crimson. She thought of the city burning, the temple pulverized to dust. And she wondered at the future, though the fear had left her, though the terror of that night had begun to fade.

The carts were continuing to rattle by, piled high with gold, as the councilors took their places on the steps, filing upward, climbing upward. Below them, the crowd of people gathered in Imperial Square was like a sea.

Julia did not know the future; no one did. She knew that for now there was peace. She knew that for now the crops yielded plenty, and the people of the city and the peninsula were well fed. She knew her fear of the law was gone; her punishment had been paid in full.

On and on the carts rattled, new carts emerging every instant. How was it possible there was so much gold in the world? None had ever seen its like.

Many had died in the wars in Eioli; many had joined the Red Hand cult and met their ends. But for now she could feel something different, something new, the Red Dawn fading, the morning hope rising. But dangers there would be, and someday the world would end as all things do.

More carts emerged and Julia felt almost exhausted. Was there no end to them? How long would the crowd stand there and wait?

But she steeled herself. She had many years ahead of her, and there was work to be done, chief among them taking care of her new family. And as she stood there she felt a kick within her stomach, and smiled.

Trumpets pealed, loud crisp trumpets. The cheering of the crowd turned from loud to deafening. The very stones of Imperial Square seemed to quake at the noise.

Her husband had appeared, yes, it was her husband, riding on the white horse of a conqueror. As he drew near his form became more visible, and her heart melted at the sight of him, at Publius, the soldier of the Empire she had loved.

In his hand was the ancient sword of the emperors, *Imperium's Rebuke,* and over his chest was a tunic gold and red, of scarlet. His face was painted crimson in the manner of the war god.

In front of him, twin servants carried a banner: *Publius*

Corvus Eiolicus, the conqueror of Eioli.

And though he'd never admit it, Julia thought he rather liked the attention of the crowd.

Behind him the train of captives walked, guarded by soldiers. Before the Temple of All Gods, at the bottom of the steps, an altar was being rolled in on wheels with a calf already tied upon the stone. And Lychicus, garbed as the Counsel of War, left his place on the steps and walked up to the altar. He drew a knife from his belt.

Before the altar, Publius stopped, and his horse reared up on its legs.

"To the gods," shouted Lychicus, "for thy provision! For granting us the victory! Remember we are mortals, their servants, always!"

After the sacrifice was attained Publius ascended the steps. His face was painted red, but she knew him well.

The cheering of the crowd was deafening as he took her hands in his. Rising, the Empire was. The Empire was rising.

And she peered into his eyes and felt whole. Publius and Julia, forever unto death. Julia and Publius, forever it would be.

Epilude

The years of Publius' reign were marked by peace and prosperity. Each season the fields produced their grain and the trees produced their fruit. The Ugar threat diminished until it was forgotten.

And on the eighth year of his reign, as was custom, Publius resigned his office and was followed by his successor. He then retired and vanished from public view, but not from mind, or memory, or heart.

I.

In the second year of Publius' reign, Julia found herself on an isolated road, covering herself in a hood for fear of being recognized.

And as she walked with purpose that wet winter morning, she questioned just what she was doing and she questioned just what she intended. But this was what she had resolved to do.

~

At the Cave of Time and Wind, the leader of the augur order met her as was arranged.

"Signora Empress," Valentius, the Wind Lord, said and bowed slightly.

She unraveled her hood, bearing her plain dress and the Star of Seladora fixed to her neck.

"I brought everything you told me to," Julia said.

She intended to give up her sorcerous powers, if she were able, and Valentius said she could. It was a choice she had arrived at after much careful thought and pained deliberation. Publius had advised her against it. But all she wanted to be was a mother to Rhea, a wife to Publius, and a manager of household affairs. Sorcery lent itself to adventure, by its very nature, and Julia had had enough adventure to fill a hundred lifetimes.

"Are you sure about this?" said Valentius. "Once done it is not easily reversed."

"I am sure," Julia said, "as I told you in my letter. I have never been more sure about anything."

But was she sure? She was sure for now, and she had thought about it for days and for weeks, through sleepless nights and long talks along the Anthans Corridor.

"Remove your necklace," said Valentius.

Julia obeyed.

"You placed your essence into this," Valentius said. "Now, you must remove your essence from it."

~

The sickness and weariness that followed lasted many days, as the augur had warned. When the fog cleared she still wondered if she had made the wrong choice. But for now, and perhaps forever, her powers were gone.

II.

In the fourth year of Publius' reign, it was a summer night, and they were in Paradise Gardens.

Publius' brother Marcus was in the Tavern drinking, as was his wont. Rhea was playing with her friend Nona at their neighbor's villa, and she and Publius were in the yard of their villa, sitting on the grass.

She was with child again and she wondered how Rhea would react to a new member of their family.

All about them were oaks, and the night was cool, and the stars glowed above-head. The moon was a white sliver and from a distant villa the sound of lute and lyre and drum were rising. Down the street there was a play underway, a classic tragedy by Anaxilas, to which they had been invited but refused.

Beside them was a bottle of wine and a plate of cheese.

"Do you feel guilty," Publius said, "being here, when the poor are going hungry in the Suburro and Mud Bottom?"

She could not remove the commoner in him, it was too deep within.

"Guilty?" Julia said. "No, though it is sad some have so much, and some so little. That is the way of life, Publius. That is the way it is and was, and the way, in some manner, it always will be."

Tomorrow she had a date with her friend Clora. They would go on a pleasure ride through the Goldenhorn Foothills. Rhea was not yet old enough to go with her.

She could tell Publius did not like this place, Paradise Gardens, but here, in the summers, she felt at rest.

III.

In the eighth year of Publius' reign, Julia sat in the Yellow Seat of the Council chamber.

"By proclamation," Publius said to Speaker Encolpius, "and according to the customs of our ancestors, I abdicate the White Throne."

At the sound of his words, Julia felt a crushing weight on her. She knew this moment had to come. Some emperors agonized over this moment; for some emperors it was difficult, but not for Publius.

In the Imperial bedchamber she found her children: Rhea, a tall auburn-headed thing at eight; Lucius, four years old and already half Rhea's size; and Caius, barely one year old, having just learned how to walk.

"We are going on a journey, children," said Julia. "It will be long."

~

In three carriages, the family and their servants began what would be a journey of weeks.

Without money from the Imperial government, Julia and Publius had known they'd need some way of making ends meet. They had fastidiously planned for this moment for years. With three children, and another on the way, they'd have many mouths to feed.

When they reached the farm they had bought, in the far northeast of the peninsula, near Latera, Julia was stunned.

The fields were overgrown with weeds, whole boards were missing from the barn, and the roof of the villa looked ready to cave in. She felt herself tear up. *How will we make it,* she wondered. *How will we do it?*

But in the months to come they planted rows of wheat and purchased chickens from their neighbors. They trimmed the olive trees in their grove and, with the help of their children, set bean seeds in the newly-ploughed soil. From the Latera market Julia bought trellises and grape seeds for the vineyard.

We will make this work… we will have it done.

IV.

In Julia's thirty-third year, a visitor came to the Corvus farm.

It was a woman she did not recognize, one with the dark hair of Publius.

And Publius dropped his hoe and shouted, "Marcella!"

It was his sister. Had she left the convent? Had she come to help them?

With all her children and with Rhea's obstinate phase, she could use all the help she could get.

V.

In Julia's seventieth year, Publius passed on.

Through tears, she helped her servants dig the pit. The body was still fresh.

But she heard a trumpet peal, and through the veil of her

tears she could see riders approaching. She wept at the sight of them, Imperial messengers. Word traveled fast.

She had thought they had been forgotten, the Imperial family from a simpler and more noble age. But they had not.

They had not forgotten, and for that reason Julia knew what their appearance meant.

She ordered the diggers to halt their work. And she drew within herself all her strength.

~

Imperial City had grown, and what had been valleys and desolate canyons were now streets lined with apartment blocks and sumptuous mansions perched on hills. Julia felt boxed in as she walked the streets, packed with people. To them she was a farmer's wife from Latera and nothing more.

In the company of her son Lucius she made arrangements at an inn. Then they waited.

The body of Publius, emperor, was turned to ash, then sealed in a limestone jar.

Julia, in Imperial Square, watched as the jar was carried into the Temple of Imperium in Imperial Square, where he would rest with all other emperors.

And then all vestige of Empress Julia was no more.

VI.

In Julia's eightieth year, she sat on the shores of the sea and listened to the whitecaps rush in. She had grown old, and her body did not work like it once did. There were aches and cramps, but she had seen so much, so much of life's joys, so much of life's tragedies.

She was wearing a straw hat and seagulls circled overhead. The farm was behind her.

She thought of Rhea, now far away. She had married a peddler from Bregantium and was now in a distant town, in a foreign land.

In her absence, Lucius, ever unmarried and ever unique, was helping with day to day things around the farm, things she once did but now could no longer do.

She felt richly blessed, but her life had not been without its hardships.

And as she sat on the shores of the sea, she thought of the night in Eioli. How long ago it was now. But the moon had been as blood, and the earth shaken by a dark fever. And she had feared such great power.

As she sat there, thinking on her life, she was grateful to have seen so much, though Publius and others were with the gods now.

And as she sat there, the sun began to sink beneath the horizon.

The skies turned red, the clouds a brilliant pink. And for a moment, just for a moment, her heart trembled.

But then she got up, and thought on what the following day would be. The pigs needed to be fed, and the grapes were almost ripe for plucking.

The twilight faded, and in the morning, the sky was a brilliant blue.

THE END

Glossary

Agornesis: One of nine large islands southwest of the peninsula.

Anaxander of Korthos: A famed general of the Eastern Kingdoms, hailing from the city-state of Korthos. He conquered the land of Khazidea and placed it under Korthian rule.

Ansolon: The founder of the first democracy in the Eastern Kingdoms, in the city of Thénai. He is considered the father of all democracies.

Anthania: A large peninsula, with the Middle Sea on its eastern edge and the ocean on its west. It is named after Anthans the Conqueror.

Anthans: The grand legate who oversaw the initial invasion of Anthania. He is sometimes called the second founder of the Empire.

Barbarian: A derogative term for a person who is neither Imperial nor from the Eastern Kingdoms.

Century: The smallest division of the Imperial army, composed of about one-hundred to two-hundred men, under the command of an official called a centurion.

Council House, the: A tower-like structure that dominates the Imperial City skyline, its construction was begun not long after the initial conquest of the Anthanian peninsula.

Cymbri, the: A warlike, mostly pastoral people of the Anthanian peninsula. Once dominant in the southeast, most have joined the Empire and lost their identity.

Donning of tunics: In the Empire, boys who reach the age of seventeen will don a tunic, often in a public ceremony. This is considered the official progression to manhood.

Eastern Kingdoms, the: A term for the rich, ancient lands of Eloesus on the opposite shore, far east across the Middle Sea.

Eioli: Considered the queen city of Ugarit, it is the region's richest and most storied city. It has dominated Ugarit for centuries.

Emperor: The leader of the empire, taking on some of the roles of a king, but heavily checked by the power of the Imperial Council.

Flamens: A secretive group of sorcerers believed to have powers of invisibility and far-sight.

Grand Legate: The commander appointed to control several legions.

Goldenhorn Mountains: Large snowcapped mountains abutting the northwestern edge of the Anthanian Peninsula. They are filled with iron mines and silver mines.

Hordo: The wife of Hordo, the founder of democracy. She was believed to be a priestess of Mira, the goddess of sunlight.

Imperial City: The largest city of the Empire, considered its heart. Its legal name is Anthans, named after the conqueror of the peninsula.

Imperial Council: A semi-democratic branch of the Imperial government, formed by thirty men voted for by the free citizens of Imperial City's thirty wards.

Imperial Guard: A force of soldiers tasked with guarding the emperor and his family.

Isle of Serpents: A large volcanic island, west from Lornatium across the sea. It is named for the many reptiles and poisonous snakes that dwell in its forests.

Kingdom of Thenoa: One of the Eastern Kingdoms, considered the most powerful after Tharta.

Khandara: A nation far south of the Empire, considered part of the Southern World. It is dominated by grassland and savannah. Despite its distance, the Empire hosts an official trading post there.

Kheroe: A city-state directly south of the Anthanian peninsula, across the sea. It is known for its strange customs and its ancient wealth. They are one of the oldest of the Empire's allies.

Knight: The lower of two tiers of the Imperial nobility. Traditionally they were seen as the Empire's soldiers, but that distinction has faded. Now, many of the Knightly class have no connections to the military.

Latera: A town in the far northeast of the peninsula.

Legate: The commander of a legion.

Legis: An expert on the procedures of the Imperial Council. He can only be overruled in certain circumstances, and even then on a two-thirds or sometimes unanimous vote.

Lornatium: A town in the far southwest of Anthania, on the coast. It began as an Eastern colony, and grew in size as the centuries progressed. Having engaged in a long war of attrition with the native Geats, it was one of the Empire's earliest allies following the invasion of the peninsula.

Middle Sea, the: An immense sea in the center of the world. The Empire lies on its westernmost edge.

Paradise Gardens: A resort town for the rich in the foothills of the Goldenhorn Mountains. Members of the Imperial Council often retreat there at the height of summer.

Rite of Spring: A celebration around the time of the spring equinox, featuring special foods, sweet cakes and gatherings. It is largely celebrated in the Empire and to a lesser extent in the Eastern Kingdoms.

Riva: A large town in central Anthania, facing the ocean, just south of the Iron Mountains.

Seladora: The goddess of woodlands, the gentle side of nature, and nymphs.

Suburro: A poor ward of Imperial City, located just outside Imperial Square.

Thartan Kingdom: One of the Eastern Kingdoms, considered the oldest and most powerful.

Ugar: A native of the land of Ugarit.

Ugarit: A land on the Anthanian peninsula's west-central coast, dominated by the three cities of Eioli, Tikal and Hoda. They are noted for their customs that are very different from the other people groups of the peninsula.

Unification. the: Considered one of the founding events of the Empire, the Unification occurred when the Formusus and Tenebarius tribes united under one king, establishing a kingdom on the island of Peregoth. A series of seven kings, called by some the Sea Kings, ruled until they were overthrown and a semi-democratic system was formed.

Urban Cohorts: The only legion that is allowed to reside in Imperial City, they are under the direct command of the Imperial Guard and the emperor. In addition to protecting the city, they act as a kind of police force, keeping the peace and upholding the law.

Ward legate: A municipal officer in each of Imperial City's wards, inferior to the councilor. His duties include overseeing elections and ensuring the smooth running of the ward government.

About the Author

Cursed at birth with a wild imagination, Andrew Cooper spent his youth dreaming of worlds more exciting than Earth.

He is a graduate of the Odyssey Writing Workshop. His stories have appeared in Morpheus Tales, Fear and Trembling, Residential Aliens and Mindflights, among others.

Contact the Author

Visit **www.aj-cooper.com** to sign up for the newsletter and stay up-to-date on new releases.

Find him on Facebook at:

www.facebook.com/AJCooperauthor